"Yes," Reynolds said, drawing the word out as he rubbed his hands together briskly, working in the lotion. I've always despised men who use hand cream. "I had a talk with the D.A. and the police commissioner and they agreed to let us handle this matter internally. The people who run this town are very aware of how much *Star Maker* contributes to the local economy. And I impressed on them that a full-scale murder investigation with all its attendant publicity could destroy the show."

I stifled the wisecrack that crouched on my tongue like a ballboy at a tennis tournament. "How long do I have? How long have you delayed production?"

Reynolds's eyes widened with alarm at the suggestion. "The season has begun. We're locked in. If I haven't made this clear, let me do it now—your activities must in no way interfere with our shooting schedule."

"You're going to keep broadcasting the show? How do you get around the fact that one of your contestants has been murdered?"

Books by David Hiltbrand

DYING TO BE FAMOUS
DEADER THAN DISCO
KILLER SOLO

DYING TO BE FAMOUS

DAVID HILTBRAND

HARPER

An Imprint of HarperCollinsPublishers

HARPER

An Imprint of HarperCollins*Publishers*
10 East 53rd Street
New York, New York 10022–5299

Copyright © 2007 by David Hiltbrand
ISBN: 978-0-06-055415-6
ISBN-10: 0-06-055415-0

First Harper paperback printing: January 2007

Printed in the United States of America

Visit Harper paperbacks on the World Wide Web at
www.harpercollins.com

10 9 8 7 6 5 4 3 2 1

To Erin,
always the Undaboss

Some people call me the Space Cowboy
Some call me the Gangster of Love
Some people call me Maurice
Cause I speak of the pompatus of love

STEVIE "GUITAR" MILLER

DYING
TO BE
FAMOUS

CHAPTER
1

Know why I hate TV? Two words: pineapple roasties.
I was in Hawaii in this glade right off the beach.
I've never been to the Aloha State but if it looks anything
like it did in this dream I was having, I'm adding it to my
must-visit list. Feather it in there alphabetically right before Iceland and Kenya.

Anyway, the sun had already set, but this bower was
well lit with torches. I was reclining in a hammock while
a trio of dusky Polynesian maidens offered me a series of
native delicacies. The girls looked like they had stepped
out of a painting by Gauguin during his *Baywatch* period.
I wrinkled my nose at each of the dishes. Everything was
a variation on poi (which, it probably goes without saying,
I've never tasted), but to me it all looked like the kind of
gruel that even Oliver Twist would turn up his smudgy
nose at.

My obdurate refusals were clearly distressing to the ladies. Pleasing me was very important to them. Finally, one smiled and said, "I know what he'll like." She whispered something to the other two, who began giggling while covering their mouths and glancing shyly at me.

A few seconds later the prescient one returned with a sizzling platter. The aroma was incredible. I already knew I'd like it; they knew I'd like it. We were all smiling. On the platter, pineapple cubes sat atop similarly sized morsels of succulent pork. Cooked above an open-pit fire, the two ingredients were fused together and lightly caramelized.

Ladies and gentlemen, I give you pineapple roasties. As far as I know, the dish does not actually exist, but in this dream, I'm telling you it was making my mouth water like Pavlov's starving aunt. The girl must have had oven mitts for hands. She picked up one of the sizzling savories and brought it over to my mouth. I opened wide and then...

The phone rang, jolting me awake. In my haze, the only things I knew for sure were that I was in my bed and it was really cold. I like to have fresh air when I'm sleeping, even in the wintertime. That may go a long way toward explaining why I still live alone. But just for the record, allow me to point out that Connecticut in January bears no relation to a Hawaiian luau.

"Hello?" I croaked.

"Jim McNamara? One minute, please. I have Mitch Reynolds on the phone for you."

And just like that, I'm pissed off. From sound asleep to resentful in five seconds. Has to be some kind of record. Even for me.

The thing is, my eyes had found the glowing numerals on the bedside clock. Not only had Mitch Reynolds woken me up at an ungodly hour—he'd delegated the job.

"Hey, Jim! How's it going, buddy?" erupted a voice in my ear—high, energetic, insinuating. But the tone was flat and distant and I could clearly hear other people arguing in the background. He had me on speakerphone. Strike four.

"Do you have any idea what time it is?" I heard how dopey I sounded. Sleepy and huffy is a pathetic mix.

"Just after midnight here in L.A.," he responded, without a trace of remorse. "Do you know who this is?"

I knew him by reputation. He was, according to the headline writers, the guy who invented reality TV. I know I was supposed to leap out of bed and salute, but as Shania sang, "That don't impress me much."

To me, Mitch Reynolds's claim to fame was about on the same level as the genius who invented pop-up ads on the Internet: They both should be shot as enemies of the state. Belay that order. Make it castrated and then shot.

I answered his question by yawning.

"Look, man," Mitch said, "we need you out here right away. The mothership has sprung a leak."

There was a long moment of silence while it became obvious to both of us that I had no idea what he was talking about.

"Star Maker!" he finally explained. "We've got a problem on the show. A big problem. The kind that requires absolute discretion. My friends in the music business tell me you can be trusted not to shoot your mouth off. And we need to keep a very tight lid on this. Look, I can't really go into specifics—or even generalities—on the phone, but we need you here pronto."

There was another pause. I got the distinct impression he was waiting for me to say, *I'm on my way!* I usually deal with rock stars, who as a breed are incredibly self-involved. But TV people make rock stars look like Samaritans.

I thought about his... well, I guess it wasn't an offer, really. Let's call it a summons.

"No," I said.

After hanging up, I unplugged the phone jack and huddled again under the covers.

I tried to burrow back into my Polynesian idyll. But no pineapple roasties for me.

What I hadn't realized is that people in the television industry don't recognize "no" as an answer. Everything is a negotiation for them. "No" isn't a refusal. It's simply a starting point, an indication that the offer isn't rich enough.

So they keep throwing money and other inducements at you until you come around. Showbiz is like a gigantic hooker convention where everyone has their price. You want Gabriel Garcia Marquez to write an episode of *Reba*? Definitely doable. You'd like Barbara Bush to play a hooker in the opening sketch of *Mad TV*? I think I have her agent's number.

"No" is merely a challenge, shorthand for, *Make it worth my while.*

I got a pretty clear picture of what I was dealing with the next morning. I was standing at the counter in my kitchen, sipping French roast and listening to Mindy Smith's CD. I like to ease into the day aurally.

I had the sports page open in front of me. We don't have a pro basketball team in Connecticut. And I try to stay regional with my rooting interests. I consider it a macrobiotic approach to sports. The problem was I hated what they had done to the Knicks and I could never root for the Celtics or any team Danny Ainge had played for.

But the year before, I had become a devoted UConn fan and both the men's and women's teams were romping through their seasons.

I was reading about the Lady Huskies' win over Villanova when there was a knock on the door. I looked at the wall clock and frowned. I'm far enough out in the country up here in Winsted that I don't get a lot of visitors. Particularly not at 8:40 in the morning.

When I opened the door, I nearly had to shield my eyes with my hand. The guy standing on the welcome mat had a smile so broad and dazzling, it was a dental klieg light. He was dressed in a uniform and matching cap modeled on a classic milkman's delivery outfit from a half century ago. Parked behind him was a cute customized minivan with "Muffin Mania" emblazoned on the side.

"Mr. McNamara?" he asked chipperly. He was holding up a big wicker basket by the handle. It was heaped with an array of his baked specialties wrapped in blue-film plastic.

Still a little overwhelmed at the early morning bounty, I merely nodded.

"This is for you," he said, handing me the basket, which turned out to be surprisingly heavy. "You have a fantastic day," he said cheerily, turning up the power on his smile to SPF 60. Then he saluted smartly and trotted off to his van.

I glanced up and down the street to see if this was some hidden-camera prank. No sign of Ashton Kutcher. So I took the package in the kitchen and unwrapped it. There was a card with a message, handwritten with exquisite calligraphy, that read: "Please Reconsider. From Mitch Reynolds and Your Friends at Tootsi Frootsi Productions."

I considered depositing the entire basket in the garbage can out in the garage. But one of those big, plump muffins—erupting with a filling of cream cheese swirled with raspberry—was calling out to me seductively.

God, it was obscenely good. But I felt so cheap and fat afterward.

I had showered and shaved and was down on my knees, asking God to keep me sober and, if it wasn't too much trouble, away from those muffins for the rest of the day when there was another knock.

Once again, a man in a uniform, but no smile this time. He worked for an overnight courier service so charming the clientele wasn't part of the mandate.

"Morning," he said, handing me a padded envelope.

"Good morning," I said, reading the shipping label.

"Sign here, please," he said, handing me a plastic "pen" nub and pointing to a line on the electronic pad he carried. Whenever I used one of those things, the result looked like a third-grader had tried to forge my signature.

"Have a good day," the courier said perfunctorily, turning back to his truck.

"You, too."

Standing on the porch, I struggled to open the package, but it was conveniently made of some impregnable polymer. It was like trying to shuck an oyster with your bare hands.

No sooner had the truck pulled out than a fire-red Toyota Celica pulled up on the shoulder in front of my house. I was the most popular guy in Connecticut. An attractive brunette got out, waved and gave me a Chelsea morning smile. She reached into the back seat of her car and pulled out a large flat carrying case by its handles. It looked like an oversized artist's portfolio. She walked toward me, carrying it, dressed in rope-belted yoga pants, a pink polo shirt and hemp sandals.

"Hi," she said. "I'm Harmony, and somebody must really like you because they bought you an ultra massage."

I considered her for a moment. "I'm sorry," I said, "but I can't accept."

"You sure? I've got the table right here," she said, patting her case. "I'm a very good masseuse."

"I'm sure you are, uh, Harmony. And I'm sorry you had to come all the way out here. But I can't."

"It's all paid for."

"I know. That's the problem."

"Okay, because if it's just a bad time you could have a rain check."

"No, thanks. I won't be needing your services."

"Okay," she said in a conciliatory voice. She looked down at the overnight envelope I held in my hands, severely mangled by all my yanking and tugging, but still sealed tight. "May I?" she asked, taking it from me. Sliding one finger into the small opening by the flap, she pulled up and the package ripped open like wet cardboard.

She handed it to me. "Have a nice day, Mr. McNamara," she said, and walked back to her car. I watched her pack up and drive off, waving as she executed a U-turn.

It's not like I wasn't tempted. I think a good massage is a pleasure fit for a king. But what if Harmony's hands started straying while she had me up on the table—naked, helpless and lubricated? What if she had been paid to throw sex into the deal? Maybe I have a dirty mind, but come on. What does "ultra massage" suggest to you? She could be like one of those evil temptresses in a James Bond film.

I wondered if I could still catch up to her and bring her back.

Kidding.

In fact, I thought she seemed legitimate, but I didn't want to take a chance. Whether or not I went to work for Mitch Reynolds—and I was still determined not to—a bought sexual encounter would compromise me irrevocably.

Why is it that my scruples always feel better in theory than in practice?

Shaking my head in grief over my lost massage, I walked back into my house and pulled out the contents of the envelope. It was a beautiful and very expensive chess set and board, made of ivory. The pieces, in a sturdy but elegant Staunton design, fit snugly in a compact carrying case.

There was another card. This one read: "Your move! Please 'check' us out—Mitch and the staff at Tootsi Frootsi."

So much for Shania. At this point, I have to admit I was impressed. The muffins—that could be a lucky guess. I mean, who doesn't like muffins? But the chess set? That was a personal touch. Somebody had done some research about my tastes.

And you have to have considerable resources to set a bribery campaign like this in motion in the middle of the night and manage to have things delivered hours later in a small town on the other side of the country.

I knew Harmony and the toothy muffin man weren't based in Winsted. That meant Tootsi Frootsi had gotten them to drive here on a moment's notice—at least from Hartford, the nearest city, but maybe from as far away as New York.

I threw some things in a gym bag and took off for the Y

before some guy showed up jangling the keys to my new Lamborghini.

It was an open gym from ten to eleven in the morning and in the dead of the winter I generally had the place to myself. I loosened up by hacking around, taking intermediate jump shots, fade-aways, reverse layups and a few hooks. Once I had a good feel for the ball, I began to work my way around the court's outer arc, throwing up three-pointers like I was doing the stations of the cross.

The internationalization of the NBA had affected my shooting ritual. I can usually tell as I release the ball if it's going in. And on those shots when my touch was good, I would bellow, "Peja Stojakovic!" like an arena announcer as the ball was airborne. When I did it right, as the ball ripped through the net, Peja's name would still be echoing in the gym.

I can't explain to you how satisfying those solitary swishes were.

Maybe it's obvious I grew up as an only child, keeping myself amused.

As I shot, I reviewed in my mind the reasons why I didn't want to go to work for Mitch Reynolds. My most recent case, helping the band Papa Roach identify the source of threats and vandalism that were plaguing a recording session, had kept me in Los Angeles for five weeks. That's about thirty-three days longer than I can stand being in that smoggy inner circle of hell. And I didn't care to go back this soon.

I wasn't sure why they were calling me in the first place. Maybe it was my status as an outsider, the perception that I wasn't tainted by Los Angeles' ratfuck ethics. But surely they knew I was a specialist. All my expertise as an investigator/troubleshooter involved the music business. If I had a business card it would restate what most people knew me as anyway:

Jim McNamara
The Rock 'n Roll Detective

Seemed to me Reynolds and his Tootsies needed to go a few pages deeper into the Yellow Pages. There had to be a TV detective in there. I pictured someone who looked like Jerry Orbach. Maybe with a young sidekick in the Parker Stevenson vein. Someone to flirt with the secretaries. Handle the heavy lifting. And absorb the occasional beating.

If I was willing to go the TV route, I didn't think I'd want to work for a schlockmeister like Reynolds. A few years ago, he was universally regarded as a Hollywood bottom feeder. He hadn't changed. The rest of the world had descended to his moronic level.

He started as the producer of crappy clip specials like *When Pets Attack* and *America's Stupidest Robbers,* filler programming put together from security camera and home video footage.

Then he came up with a colossally stupid concept, *Beauty and the Beast,* a hybrid between a dating and a game show in which a dozen supermodel types schemed and connived to be selected by a lumpy-looking schlub as his dream date. The prize was $100,000, but the real inducement was weeks of network face-time. Mitch's great discovery—one that pitted the complexion of prime time—was that nowadays people will engage in any kind of degrading behavior in order to be on television. To paraphrase Randy Bachman: Any fame is good fame.

Of course, *Beauty and the Beast*'s winner, a honey-haired, leggy Southern beauty with a dazzling smile, dumped the bum as soon as the cameras were turned off. But it caused a quantum shift in network programming. The series did only moderately well, but it was made for next to nothing. In TV land, that's a grand slam.

Mitch followed that up with *Fatal Fiancé* and *Monster-in-Law*. In the former, a bevy of very attractive young women competed to be the chosen one of a guy in the final throes of a mysterious but not contagious disease. Like *Beauty and the Beast,* it was a catfight masquerading as a romance.

But it was bizarrely morbid. The guy made a deathbed proposal. If the girl accepted, she won a big cash prize. Then came the twist: He wasn't really sick. He had been faking the symptoms. Would she agree to marry him now for double the prize money, knowing he would live? She enthusiastically said yes. How could she not? Deception was such a good foundation on which to build an engagement. But oddly enough, they never made it to the altar. That made the batting average for these TV will-you-marry-me shows roughly 0-for-forever.

I read somewhere that the *Fatal Fiancé* winner was now a weathergirl down in Phoenix. That must be a pretty cushy gig. "It's ninety-five degrees here in the Valley of the Sun. Again."

Monster-in-Law focused on a couple in which the guy was totally smitten with the girl. Hardly surprising. She was gorgeous and classy, clearly way out of his league. The drawback was her family, played by actors, who were coached to be as boorish and intrusive as possible. Could the girl coax her victim all the way to the marriage ceremony with her "kin" doing everything imaginable to sabotage the deal?

For some reason, the prospective groom never questioned the camera crews constantly orbiting around him, capturing the smallest details of his wedding preparations.

I don't know what any of these programs had to do with reality. But that's what they were dubbed. I preferred to think of them as Shun TV because they all traded in seduction, manipulation and humiliation.

Like a choking vine, Reynolds's grotesque creations slowly took over more and more of Fox's schedule. The fact that the network seemed to have lost all ability to develop a halfway engaging drama or sitcom helped the spread of this mutant form of entertainment. The other networks jumped on the bandwagon like hippos in heat. Imitation being the sincerest form of television.

Appointed president of specials and alternative programming, more and more power gravitated to Reynolds until he was the de facto head of the network. That was like putting the bathroom attendant in charge of a fancy restaurant.

Of course, who am I to question the wisdom of the networks? They've been running the business into the ground for thirty years without any help from me.

Until I got the call to arms in the middle of the night, I wasn't aware that *Star Maker* was part of Reynolds's fiefdom. Like the vast majority of his shows, it was blatantly stolen from a concept that had proven successful overseas. In this case, England.

Star Maker was a simple talent show that had grown into a monster. A group of young amateur singers, selected by a trio of musical experts, competed against each other, with the viewing audience calling in to vote for their favorites. One by one, the contestants were sent packing until the last remaining singer was crowned a star and awarded a recording contract.

I had checked out the show about midway through the first season as the buzz around it started to build. Looked like bad karaoke to me and I had tuned in only sporadically and unintentionally since.

One of the major turnoffs for me was the material, a gooey procession of bathetic ballads and maudlin R&B. It was like the playlist from one of those god-awful MOR stations, the kind that offers "the greatest hits of the sixties, seventies and eighties."

The Buggles were wrong. It wasn't video that killed the radio star. It was oldies. Is there anything sadder than misplaced nostalgia?

Radio had abandoned its greatest asset: being current. They shouldn't be playing songs from last month, much less last year. Remember the excitement of waiting for the disc jockey to play that contagious new song? Probably not. Radio has become a graveyard. Move along, folks; nothing to listen to here.

The thing is, *Star Maker* didn't even swipe the staples of the soft oldies format like Phil Collins and Billy Joel. Instead it ravaged the bones of forgotten one-hit hacks trying to sound like Phil and Billy. Of course, the kids on the show were way too young to be familiar with this stale mush, so they couldn't even fake it. The result was bad singers singing bad songs with absolutely no feel for the material.

But hey, what do I know? *Star Maker,* which was just starting its fifth season, was a certified smash, absolutely dominant in the two nights it aired.

As I left the Y, I wondered what the emergency could be on the show and why they felt the need to bring me in.

I drove over to my buddy Ken's diner for an early lunch. His iced tea leaves something to be desired, but he's an artist when it comes to egg salad on rye toast. Ken refuses to divulge the secret ingredient, but I suspect he's adding a soupçon of Miracle Whip.

As I waited for my order, I leafed through a number of papers left by the breakfast crowd, including the *New York Times* and *USA Today*, but there were no scandalous items involving *Star Maker*.

On the way back to my car, I did a little window-shopping. My mother's birthday was coming up. I was a reasonably dutiful but far from solicitous son, a failing which she managed to remind me of in almost every conversation we had.

When I got home, there was a limousine parked by my mailbox. A liveried gentleman stood deferentially on my porch. He held his gray hat by its black visor in one hand and an envelope in the other. The windows in the limo were tinted, so I couldn't tell if anyone was seated inside.

The driver bowed slightly as I walked up the path. "Good afternoon, sir," he said. "This is for you." I took the envelope from him. My name was hand-printed on the front. "I've been instructed to wait for a reply," he said.

"Would you like to come in while I read it?" I asked, unlocking the front door.

"I'd as soon wait out here, if you don't mind."

I let myself in and closed the door behind me. Standing in the foyer, I ripped open the envelope. As I unfolded the letter within, a piece of blue paper fluttered to the ground, landing face up. It was a certified check for $50,000.

"Please consider this check a retainer," read the letter. "Because time is of the absolute essence, I will double this bonus if you will pack a few things and let this driver take you directly to the airport. I will also double your going rate for every day you work for me. Looking forward, Mitch Reynolds."

I opened the door. "Be with you in a jiffy, " I said to the man on the porch.

"Very good, sir."

Then I set about packing. As usual, I spent more time sifting through my CDs than I did on my wardrobe.

And yes, I'm very aware of what slutty sorority my acceptance put me in. In fact, as I was digging clothes out of my closet, I thought of George Bernard Shaw's quip: "We've already established what you are, ma'am. Now we're just haggling over the price."

So don't start with me. I have bills to pay. Same as you. And I don't want to be following snot-nosed punk rockers around when I'm fifty.

After the flight to Los Angeles, which typically left me feeling as if I had just spent five hours being trampled in Pamplona, I was met by another driver waiting outside the security checkpoint.

After settling me in the back seat of his gleaming sedan, he started the car and then turned to face me over his shoulder. "I'm to drive you directly to the studio, if that's all right with you, Mr. McNamara."

"Fine," I said. As if I had a choice.

We took the 101 to the 5 East and got off at Fairfax Avenue, driving north to the gates of Television City, a honeycomb of executive offices and soundstages all dominated by one squat but massive building.

A long line of people in gaudy tourist wear hugged one side of the building.

"Do you know what they're waiting for?" I asked.

The driver glanced over. "Audience members on *The*

Price is Right," he said, pulling up to the front entrance. "They're out here every day."

I thanked him and walked inside, feeling conspicuous with my bags. Three uniformed receptionists sat behind an imposing console in the lobby, flanked by armed security guards.

I'll take receptionist number three, Bob, I thought, announcing myself to the one on the right. He looked down at a console. I'm pretty good at reading upside down, but the screen was tilted so visitors couldn't see its contents.

"Mr. Reynolds is in the Archie Bunker Conference Room on the second floor," he said, handing me a pass and smiling. "Take a right and then another right as you come out of the elevator. Bear left at the Miss Hathaway Screening Room. You can't miss it."

The directions were right as far as they went, but they left out the quarter mile of corridor I had to traverse before reaching the Bunker bunker.

I knocked and a young woman opened the door in an odd crouched posture. I thought perhaps an Igor-like hunchback had been appointed the gatekeeper, but then I realized she was sitting so close to the door, she only had to half rise to reach the handle.

The room was hazy with stale cigarette smoke. Bottles of designer water, coffee cups and phone consoles were scattered across the conference table, around which sat three men in leather master-and-commander chairs. A row of modest cloth chairs lined the walls, forming a second perimeter around the table. Ms. Igor and two other attentive but frazzled young people sat in the outer ring.

I stood in the doorway, weighed down with bags. I thought of Keith Richards, cooing "Honey, I'm home," as he enters another empty hotel room in the Rolling Stones' tour documentary *Cocksucker Blues.*

"Jim?" called out the man at the head of the table eagerly. He looked like a Woodstock pixie: small and slight with big, burning eyes and even bigger hair emanating out from his head in frizzy, tightly coiled ringlets. He reminded me of excruciatingly precious seventies pop singer Leo Sayer.

I nodded.

"I'm Mitch," he said. "Glad you could join us." It's always nice when the client is happy to see me. Usually doesn't last long. Things tend to go south in a hurry.

"About bloody time," said the man to Mitch's left, glaring at me. See, that didn't take long. He was the only person in the room I recognized. Rodney Hampden, *Star Maker*'s arrogant and acerbic judge, was the show's real star. He had been just an obscure British record executive until he was appointed to the judging panel on *Pop Star*, the British template for *Star Maker*. Hampden's decimating comments to the contestants were considered such a crucial component in the program's success that he was imported over here along with the format.

He had made himself right at home on our shores. Like a Mediterranean fruit fly.

Hampden had a bristle of jet-black hair that reminded me of the video game character Sonic the Hedgehog. His face was handsome, despite its perpetually bitter expression. In five years on the air, no one had ever seen him smile.

He was giving me his usual bullying look, as if my very existence were an affront to the natural order of the universe. It was intended to make you feel like a bag lady at the opera house.

"Be nice, Rodney," murmured the man facing him across the table, with a distinct British accent. Actually, the way the guy was slumped over so far in his chair, he seemed to be facing his own navel. He was the senior member of the *Star Maker* brain trust, with a nimbus of silver hair framing a severely rutted face. He was the only one at the table formally dressed, if you overlooked his jarringly loud red-striped shirt.

I have pretty good radar for telling when people are chemically altered. And this guy was shit-faced. I was willing to bet that wasn't Sprite in the tumbler he kept a tight grip on.

"Jim McNamara, I'm sure you know Rodney Hampden," said Reynolds. I nodded at Rodney. He scowled back as if we were two boxers who had just been introduced prior to a twelve-round fight. Let's get ready to rumble.

"And this is Ian Braithwait, *Star Maker*'s executive producer," continued Reynolds. The white-haired gent was too soused to lift his chin off his chest, but he managed to wave two fingers on his free hand in greeting. The assistants didn't rate introductions.

"Put your things down and take a seat," said Reynolds, settling back in his chair. "I'd like to get you up to speed as quickly as possible." Then he paused. "Actually, I'm not sure where to start."

Rodney snorted. "It's bloody simple, isn't it, mate?" he said, rising and making a circuit of the table away from me. His Nordic-looking assistant immediately jumped to her feet and trailed him. "Our golden boy Matt has been murdered. You're to find out who did it." He stopped in his steps for added emphasis. "But mostly you're charged with making sure it fucking well doesn't happen again." He moved determinedly toward the door.

"Where are you going, Rodney?" asked Reynolds.

"You lot can deal with this. I'm leaving," he said belligerently. "I've been cooped up in this bloody room for the better part of two days. I've missed two rounds of golf.

If I hurry I can still get in nine holes today." Then he was gone, his beautiful factotum scurrying behind him.

"Well," said Reynolds, exhaling. "Rodney certainly gets right to the point, doesn't he?"

"It's his gift," muttered Braithwait.

I lifted the straps on my bags off my shoulders and lowered them to the ground, taking a seat. This was a story I wanted to hear.

CHAPTER
5

It's essentially as Rodney described it," Reynolds said, steepling his fingers under his chin. Now he looked like a devotional Leo Sayer. "One of our contestants, Matthew Hanes, has been murdered."

"How and when?" I asked. Sergeant Joe Friday got nothin' on me.

"Two nights ago—Wednesday. He was asphyxiated in his hotel room. Actually, we believe he was drugged and then asphyxiated."

"Is that what you think or what the police say?" I asked.

He spread his hands, as if to say, *Does it matter?*

"Tell me with more detail."

"Well, it was right after our first live show of the season when we announced the finalists," began Reynolds. "Most of the kids went out to celebrate, but Matt went back to the hotel. It was his last night there. He was supposed to move into the Star Mansion yesterday."

That was one of *Star Maker*'s central conceits. The finalists all lived in a house together and became the closest and dearest friends imaginable. Meanwhile, they were engaged in doing everything in their power to eliminate each other.

Reynolds lowered his chin and shook his head, disconsolate at life's cruel ironies. Then, his mini-display of sadness concluded, he looked back up at me. "Anyway, apparently Matt and his roommate had a habit of getting a late-night pizza delivered. The roomie was sent home last week, but I guess Matt kept up the midnight snack tradition. Someone sprinkled enough Rohypnol on top of the pepperoni to paralyze a horse. Then, when he was out of it, they put a pillow over his face until he stopped breathing."

The chemical he was referring to is commonly known as the date-rape drug. Its street name, in pill form, is roofies.

"How do you know the drug was on the pizza?"

"Police lab analyzed it. There were still five slices left in the box. And they tested Matt's blood."

"And what makes you sure a pillow was used?"

"It was lying right by his body. The crime scene tech found Matt's hair and skin fibers all over the pillowcase fabric. He said the pillow was pressed down so hard on his face it was like a death mask."

"Any suspects?"

Reynolds shook his head emphatically. His hair didn't seem to move. "Matt didn't have an enemy in the world, far as we can tell. Great kid. And I mean that."

"So what do you want from me?"

He looked at me with surprise shading on disappointment. "Find the killer, make sure it doesn't happen to anyone else," he said, as if he were stating the obvious.

"I have a feeling LAPD may resent the intrusion."

He shook his head. "I've asked them to stand down. You'll be point man on this investigation." He flipped up his palm behind his ear, and his assistant sprang into action. I had identified her as Igor, but she looked like a young Michelle Pfeiffer. I thought she was going to slap some telling document or photograph in his hand, but she pulled out an opalescent bottle from her belly pack and pumped three squirts of unguent onto his palm.

"The LAPD dropped a homicide? On your say-so?"

"Yes," he said, drawing the word out as he rubbed his hands together briskly, working in the lotion. He looked to me like a raccoon washing its food. Of course, I've always despised men who use hand cream. "I had a talk with the DA and the police commissioner and they agreed to let us handle this matter internally."

"Really?" I know I sounded skeptical, but I was in fact dumbfounded.

"Yes, really. I think the piece you're missing here is this is a company town."

"How green was my valley," intoned Braithwait, apropos of nothing I could discern.

"The people who run this town are very aware of how much *Star Maker* contributes to the local economy," continued Reynolds. "And I impressed on them that a full-scale murder investigation with all its attendant publicity could destroy the show.

"They are quite willing for us to pursue it," he said. His hand-wringing finished, he looked at me with the grim focus of a bird locking in on a worm. For the first time, I saw the sharpie beneath Reynolds's Malibu-mellow surfer-boy act. "Of course, I guaranteed you would get results."

I stifled the wisecrack that crouched on my tongue like a ball boy at a tennis tournament. "How long do I have?"

"Pardon?"

"How long have you delayed production?"

Reynolds's eyes widened with alarm at the suggestion. Even Braithwait executed a sloppy approximation of the sign of the cross with his left hand. "The season has begun. We're locked in. If I haven't made this clear, let me do it now—your activities must in no way interfere with our shooting schedule."

"You're going to keep broadcasting the show?" I know, I know. He had already made his intentions abundantly clear, but I was still incredulous.

"There was never any question," Reynolds said. "That's why you're here, Jim. I wanted someone who could work this without disrupting the show."

"How do you get around the fact that one of your contestants has been murdered? Isn't that going to take some of the attention away from the singing?" There was a little more sarcasm in my voice than I meant to display.

"We don't acknowledge it. We simply say Matt left the show. No biggie. We lose a couple of finalists every season." That was true. But it was usually because one of the "kids" had an extensive criminal record revealed on the Smoking Gun website. Or a fan of their early pornography work couldn't resist sharing.

"How about the press?"

He gave a dismissive wave with his skin-so-soft hand. "Taken care of. We put an item in *USA Today*, spinning the story the way we want it. They're practically our house organ. They'll print anything we tell them."

"Aren't you afraid of being sued? This kid, Matt, died in your employ."

My question caused Reynolds and Braithwait to erupt

in the kind of helpless laughter a stand-up comic would do anything to hear.

"Ohhhh," said Reynolds, still chuckling while reaching up to wipe his eye. "The short answer is no, we're not afraid. If you could see the contracts these kids sign to get on the show...Let's just say we're indemnified from everything. And I mean everything. We could execute the losers in prime time instead of sending them home and they still couldn't bring legal action."

"What about the dead kid's family?"

"Taken care of. One of our lawyers sat down with Matt's parents and pointed out their negligible legal options. Then he offered them a very generous cash settlement. And I had an around-the-world cruise left over from my *Joe Convict* show. Mr. and Mrs. Hanes are steaming towards the South Pacific as we speak. They return the week after we crown the next Star. By then, they should be fairly far along in the bereavement process."

"'Tis a far, far better thing..." added Braithwait, his chin resting on his chest.

"What if one of the finalists blows the whistle after they're eliminated?"

"A possibility," Reynolds conceded. "But a remote one. The nondisclosure clauses in the contract are very clear and highly punitive. But even more important, anyone who leaks doesn't get to go on the post-show concert tour. *And* they'll be blackballed in the music industry. All of them are too ambitious to risk that." He paused. "Any other concerns?"

I couldn't think of any. Then again, I was so blown away by how tightly controlled this situation was, I couldn't think of much. So I shook my head.

"Good," said Reynolds, rising. Igor the Supermodel rose behind him. Braithwait's assistant came over and basically

lifted him out of the chair. Now I understood why the soz-
zled Brit was the only one with a male helper. "We'll leave
this in your hands. You will have the full cooperation of
everyone on the show."

"Happy hunting, old boy," said Braithwait. His assistant
nudged him out the door as if he were a large, very drunk
marionette.

I sat for a second to take stock of the surreal situation.
By the time I gathered up my bags and walked out the
door, there was no sign of my hiring committee. I looked
up and down the long, empty corridors. They were gone.

And so the renowned detective faced the first serious
challenge in this baffling case: how to find his way back
to the lobby.

CHAPTER 6

One thing I learned that afternoon: If you hit the Carol Burnett Editing Center, you've gone too far.

When I eventually regained the lobby, I approached the same receptionist I'd talked with when I'd arrived, figuring we had already established a relationship.

"Neither Mr. Reynolds nor Mr. Braithwait have offices in this complex," he said in toneless response to my inquiry.

"But I just met with them upstairs."

He merely looked at me, as if he had said everything that needed to be mentioned.

"I don't understand," I said.

He shot his eyes over his shoulder at the security guard as if to say, *You believe this guy?* The guard tucked his head down, inflating his chins, his hands crossed on his belly.

"Their show shoots here," he said with a hint of condescension. "But their production office is over in Universal City. And I saw both their limos leave a few minutes ago."

"Thanks," I said, wanting to throttle the guy. I walked outside, set my bags down and looked around blankly, weighing my options.

I felt well and truly marooned. No car, no lodgings, no particular place to go. If I had a cell phone, at least I'd have something to throw in disgust. My only consolation was that I was on the clock.

Picking up my stuff, I made the long walk through the parking lot to the gate and headed south down Fairfax. I thought I had spotted a hotel across the street from the Farmers Market on my way in.

I was right, but I couldn't shake the air of make-believe that seemed to have engulfed me. The hotel was called the Farmer's Daughter. Everything was decorated in calico, gingham and chintz. The entire staff—the doormen, the front desk clerks, the concierge—was dressed in overalls.

"Howdy," said the smiling young man who checked me in, the singsong greeting a halfhearted imitation of Minnie Pearl.

The rustic theme continued in my room, which resembled a set from *Petticoat Junction*, right down to its splatter-ware washbasin. Two things I liked: They pulled off the barnyard illusion with élan. Style points for that. And beneath its home-baked crust, my room was stocked with the most modern amenities.

The only elements I require in a hotel room are a shower with decent water pressure and a high-speed Internet connection. Satisfied on both fronts, I kicked off my shoes and decided to set a spell.

Once I was semi-settled in, I called my AA sponsor Chris Towle at his home in Pennsylvania. Strictly speaking, I should probably have replaced Chris years ago with a sponsor who lived near me in Connecticut, because the relationship generally implies regular face-to-face meetings. But Chris was my first sponsor back when I was getting sober in New York, and I had held on to him even after we both moved out of the city.

We kept in close touch by phone and that worked well for me. Although not on this evening.

"You took another job in Los Angeles?" he asked with a little more alarm than I felt the situation called for.

"It so happens that a lot of the music industry is based out here."

"Really? I wasn't aware." Uh-oh. Heavy sarcasm. This wasn't going well at all.

Obviously, Chris was more knowledgeable about rock 'n roll than me. I had merely worked for a record company, before a nasty heroin habit took me down. He had created some of the genre's undisputed masterpieces as the reclusive leader of Risen Angels.

In recent years, journalism has fallen in love with the list. Everywhere you look, it's the "50 Best" this and the "10 Worst" that. The ranking of things allows you to make a bold, authoritative statement in an extremely labor-relaxed fashion. You simply write down your favorites and put numbers in front of them. Since journalists tend to be both lazy and opinionated as hell, lists are a godsend.

The point is, whenever you see one of those cover stories on the "100 Greatest Albums of All Time," you'll invariably find one or both of the Risen Angels' records included, usually in the top ten.

So explaining to Chris Towle how the music business works isn't a smart idea.

"You've never had a problem with Los Angeles before," I wheedled.

He snorted with what sounded very much like derision. "Maybe you haven't been listening," he said. "Outside of Las Vegas, I think it may be the most craven, materialistic city on the planet. It's the worst possible atmosphere for you." I started to argue, but he cut me off. "Addicts like you and me are creatures of habit, Jim. We thrive on routine—morning prayers, regular meetings, early to bed, all that good stuff. It seems like you're drawn towards chaos and excitement and glamour. That worries me. And it should worry you."

I thought about what my sponsor said. I loved the guy to death, but that didn't mean he was always right. I thought the concern was misplaced. I know I didn't deserve the lecture.

"Chris?"

"Yeah."

"Are you okay?"

There was a long silence. Then I heard him exhale through his nose. "No. You're right," he said. "I'm all twisted up about this kid at work." Chris was a counselor on the adolescent wing of a drug and alcohol rehab near his farm on the fringes of the Poconos. "He's a smart kid from some town in Maryland. Sensitive as hell and cursed with a lifetime supply of defiance. He gets out in a couple of days and I know he's not ready.

"I met his mom when she came up for family week. No help there. I keep trying to break through to him, but I'm running out of time. That's why I'm a little testy. Sorry, Jim."

Ah, the magic words.

That's one of the reasons I love people in recovery. We have this nifty little gift called the 10th Step. Encourages us to take stock of our behavior, sometimes in mid-rant, and admit when we're wrong. Seems to me most civilians go through life with blinders on, unable and unwilling to look at the harm—both venal and cardinal—they do to others.

How many prompt, voluntary apologies do you get from that rude co-worker or the sister-in-law who gets on your nerves? Not nearly enough, I'll tell you that. Maybe this is a vestige of growing up in a boozy Irish Catholic family where blame was always assigned and never accepted, but to me, the sweetest phrase in the language is a freely offered "I'm sorry."

"So what are you out there working on?" Chris asked. "Helping Slash find his stash?"

"Actually, for once I'm not working for a musician. I've been hired by a TV show. I don't know if you've heard of it—*Star Maker*."

"Are you kidding? That piece of shit is one of the biggest headaches we have at the rehab."

"You're kidding."

"No. You know we want these kids concentrating on their issues while they're here. So their TV viewing is restricted."

"Right."

"Well, we let the kids pick one show they can watch outside the usual hours. It breaks down on gender lines. The boys usually vote for *Pimp My Ride*. Actually they really want *Chappelle's Show*, but that has problematic content.

"The girls always pick *Star Maker*. At least during its season, which I guess is starting up again. God, they'd riot if we didn't let them watch it. Somehow they've convinced these girls that if they don't vote for their favorite—and vote often—their choice will lose.

"We take away all their cell phones when they check in, but that doesn't stop them. When an episode of *Star Maker* ends, they fan out all over the facility, even breaking into offices to get to phones to vote. It's wild, like the scene where the slaves revolt in *Spartacus*.

"We had pass codes to get an outside line, but they kept finding them out and sharing them, so we went to these cumbersome manual locks. They still try to smash those off, but they end up destroying the whole console. That show costs us a couple of hundred dollars a week in repairs."

I whistled, a descending glissando, to signify my astonishment.

"So why does *Star Maker* need your services, Gentleman Jim?"

I explained to him how Matt Hanes had been murdered, with the caveat that this was confidential because the producers were intent on covering it up.

"Wow. Do you think one of the other contestants killed him?"

"I don't know. I just got here."

"Are you planning to use Whitey?"

"Probably, yeah." Whitey was a legendary AA figure in Los Angeles. Chris had introduced me to him nearly two years ago, and now whenever I had a case in southern California, I recruited Whitey. Best leg man a detective could ask for. Whitey knew everybody.

"You know he'll go nuts if you start working out there and don't call him to help. It's all Whitey talks about. I think he has some deep-seated Humphrey Bogart fantasy going on that you help him fulfill."

"I feel bad using him, though, Chris. I keep telling him to keep track of the hours, but he won't accept money from me. Twice now after he's worked with me I've written him checks that he hasn't cashed."

Chris laughed. "Whitey doesn't need your money. He'd pay you for letting him feel like Sam Spade."

"Where's his money come from?"

"Ask him when you see him. And tell him I said hello. Oh, and Jim?"

"Yeah?"

"Make sure he takes you to meetings."

No worries there. Without regular attendance at AA meetings, the City of Angels was unbearable. With them, it was merely a nightmare.

CHAPTER

7

I don't know if my mattress at the Farmer's Daughter was stuffed with goose down or cornhusks or some other secret pastoral substance, but I slept like a log.

Early the next morning I wandered across Fairfax to the Farmers Market and sat at a counter, sipping java, watching the shops in the market get ready for the day ahead. The sunlight was slanted and enchanted. Deliverymen wheeled in carts stacked with boxes, people hosed down the areas in front of their stores and set up tables or display racks. It was an hour when I actually enjoyed Los Angeles—before it was open for business. Let me clarify that: It was the only hour when I enjoyed Los Angeles. I suppose that if you got rid of ninety-five percent of the population, it might be a decent place.

There had been a *USA Today* outside the door of my hotel room and I had just finished perusing the basketball scores when an item on the front page of the Life section caught my eye. The headline read: "*Star Maker* Favorite Withdraws."

The text announced that "Matt Hanes, heartthrob and early frontrunner in this season's *Star Maker* competition, has abruptly pulled out of the hit singing contest to deal with 'an unfortunate family situation,' according to a spokesman for the show." There was even a quote from Matt in which he apologized to his fans and expressed a hope that he might audition for next year's show. That would be a neat trick. At the conclusion of the item (I can't bring myself to refer to pieces in *USA Today* as articles), it mentioned that Hanes had been replaced by Greg Jeffers, the final runner-up to the Top Ten.

Wherever he was, Joseph Pulitzer must have been very proud.

Back in my room, I showered and shaved and then looked up Tootsi Frootsi Productions in the phone book. I dialed the number, asking to be connected with Mitch Reynolds. The operator asked who was calling and then parked me on hold for so long I could have had my hair braided.

Finally a breathless young woman in an agitated state got on the line. "Oh, my God," she said, spacing the words out as if she were counting in a game of hide-and-seek. "Where are you? I've been going out of mind looking all over for you since yesterday. Listen, before we go any further, give me your cell number."

"I don't have a cell phone."

"Excuse me?" she said, as if I had just suggested she take off all her clothes and rub the phone against her body.

"Don't have one."

"Please don't joke with me, Mr. McNamara. I'm in enough trouble already for letting you slip off yesterday. I need to be able to get ahold of you at a moment's notice—day or night. So just give me your cell number. Please."

I'm sorry," I said. "But who is this?"

"Oops, my bad. This is Roxie. Roxie Bena. I'm your assistant."

Now it was my turn to be flabbergasted. "My assistant?"

"That's right. And there's something we should get straight right away. When you disappear like this, you know who gets blamed, don't you?"

"First of all," I said, "I didn't disappear, Roxie. Mitch and Ian walked out on me and left me alone in that conference room without any instructions or contacts. And second of all, I seriously do not own a cell phone."

"My God, how do you..." I'm pretty certain the next word out of her mouth was going to be "live." But she pulled up in time. "Why don't I get you one? That can be the first order of business."

"No, thank you."

"How about a pair of walkie-talkies? They have surprising range these days."

"Nope. I just want to know where to report to work."

"Well, usually this is the day the kids go on location to shoot the car promos, but everything has been backed up because of, well, you know. So everybody is going over to the studio. They're doing song selections for this week's show. Do you know where the studio is?"

"Yes."

"Do you want me to send a car? Or I could pick you up?"

"No. I'll walk over."

"Walk?" she asked, as if I had suggested something outlandish, like riding a yak over to the studio.

"Yeah, that process where you put one foot in front of the other?"

"You know, Mr. McNamara, I was pretty happy when they told me you were straight-edge. No drugs or drinking. 'Cause usually my job is to assist the celebrity judges, and some of them are completely whacked out. But you may be the weirdest person I've worked for yet."

"I'm not sure what to say to that, Roxie."

"What time will you be there?"

"In twenty minutes. Could you please make sure my name is on the entry list? And let's set in motion whatever ID I need so that I can come and go at the studio and at Tootsi Frootsi."

"That I can do."

"See you soon."

The last thing I wanted was an assistant. I didn't need someone to cater to my needs. In my own mind, I'm Lone Wolf McQuade.

Besides, the whole concept of having a helper hovering around struck me as hideously extravagant, the modern-day equivalent of being a slave owner. But I figured it wouldn't hurt to have someone in my corner who worked on the show and knew all the players. I just didn't want her hovering too close.

Of course, that was before I met Roxie.

When I walked up to the TV complex, there was another line of exuberant tourists standing in the sun, waiting for *The Price Is Right*. Inside the main building, the receptionist examined his screen and immediately directed me back to the *Star Maker* set, which entailed walking outside and about a half mile east to the Larry Hagman Theater. People in golf carts whizzed past me in both directions on the footpath.

A pretty Latina page stood inside the entrance checking

IDs. She was flanked by a pair of hulking guards. Roxie had gotten my name on the visitor list and I was permitted to enter, right after one of the guards, the one who looked like Orlando Pace, gave me the once-over with a handheld metal detector. The thick device looked like an electric toothbrush in his hand.

I walked into the theater, which I recognized from my brief sampling of the show. The seats were empty, but up on the stage, a half dozen workers scurried around attending to equipment.

To stage right, I knew, was the red room, where on show night, the contestants awaited their turn to perform, surrounded by blatant product placement reminders of their soft drink sponsor. Just to make sure you got the point, giant cups emblazoned with the soda's logo were parked in front of the judges during each show as well. I think *Star Maker* was about a season away from letting the sponsors just tattoo the contestants' foreheads. The show obviously was using NASCAR as its marketing model.

To stage left was a double pair of doors, both hanging open, with the sound of music pouring out. I walked down the aisle and through the doors into a large rehearsal space. Across the room to my left was a corridor down which I could see dressing rooms. At the back of the right side of the room was a large and bustling wardrobe department, with row after row of outfits on hangers. In front of me was a petite Hispanic kid with prominent cheekbones, his long black hair slicked down and shaped into spit curls à la Prince.

He was standing by a piano, holding a microphone and singing the chorus of "I Want a New Drug." But his voice was way too high and thin for the song, and his careful enunciation of all the lyrics made his delivery sound ridiculously stiff.

This is pop music, son—I fought the urge to yell at him.

You have to slur the words. "Louie, Louie" is one of the genre's only enduring works precisely because no one can understand the lyrics. You're never going to get anywhere if you're actually going to pronounce this crap. Where's the mystery in that?

A hefty middle-aged woman with light coffee skin and a big bouquet of hair held back with a scrunchie was watching the singer and wincing with every line. Finally she signaled to the pianist to stop banging out the chords.

"Ricky, Ricky," she said, when the music died. "It's not working for you, babe."

"C'mon, Sandy," he said in a high, querulous voice. "You gotta let me have this one. I know I can make it work."

"Trust me. You can't. Let's move down the list. There's other songs better suited to your voice. Why don't we try 'If This Is It'? That's a song you could shine on."

"But this is the one I wanna do. Pleaaaase, Sandy." In addition to his annoying manner, he had a pronounced lisp. As he continued to plead his case, I made my way over to one of the folding chairs lined up against the wall.

No sooner had I sat down than a young woman dropped into the seat next to me. Leaning sideways toward me, she whispered out of the side of her mouth, "Don't forget to turn off your cell phone."

"I don't have one," I started to say, and then looked over at her. She was smiling impishly.

"Roxie?" I asked

"Morning," she said like a bad ventriloquist. My assistant had blond hair with dark highlights that fell in tight waves to her shoulders. Her face was plump and very pretty, with big blue eyes above ripe cheeks. She was wearing a navy blue polo shirt, showing strong arms. Roxie was medium height, but buxom and athletic-looking.

"Do we have to whisper?" I whispered.

"Say WHAT?" she said loudly. When I shied back, startled, she laughed and slapped my shoulder. "Just kidding. Etiquette in the rehearsal room is to stay quiet when they're singing. Otherwise we can talk as much as we want.... So where are you staying anyway?"

"Right down the street at the Farmer's Daughter."

"Is that a hotel?"

"Yes. Never heard of it?"

She shrugged. "Mostly the people I deal with stay in hotels that have either the words 'Regency' or 'Bel Air' in them. But that's a really weird coincidence."

"What is?"

"Farmer's daughter. That's what they used to call me when I first got to Los Angeles."

"No kidding. Where you from, Roxie?"

"Iowa. Near Davenport. But my dad was a school principal, not a farmer."

"Is Roxie your real name?"

Her eyebrows went up with surprise at the question, as if I had guessed her secret. She leaned toward me again. We were back to whispering. "No. It's Hannah. Hannah Hickenlooper." She checked my face intently for signs of mirth. "But that's the whole point of this town. You get to reinvent yourself."

I flicked my chin over to the entrance to the wardrobe area, where the woman was still trying to give constructive criticism to the young singer. "So who do we have here?"

She looked over at the pair. "That's Ricky. Ricky Tavares. He's one of the finalists. He's talking to Sandy Bauer. I guess at the moment he's arguing with her. She's the voice coach. She helps all the contestants pick their material and then works with them during the week on their performance."

"Why does he care so much about a crappy song like 'I Want a New Drug'?"

"Shhhh!" she said, looking around worriedly. "Rule number one: Never make fun of the material."

"Why not?"

"Because it will only get worse," she said, smirking. "This is the day when there's usually the most tension, particularly at this stage in the competition, when there's ten finalists and they all need songs. It gets easier as we go along. But right now, the pickings can get pretty slim. No one wants to get stuck with a clunker. You catch a bad song and you're gone."

"So why is he fighting for 'I Want a New Drug'?"

"Because it's Huey Lewis week."

I leaned back to digest that. I had forgotten that once the *Star Maker* finalists were selected, each week's sing-off was arranged around a theme. I'm sure that after four seasons, it was hard not to repeat yourself. But Huey freakin' Lewis?

"So who's around today?" I asked eventually.

"All the finalists should be here. They all vanned over together from the house this morning." She leaned in again. "There's no love lost among this bunch."

"I want to meet everyone. Have they been told who I am and what I'm here to do?"

She looked around the room, then leaned in close to my ear. "They were told a private investigator was being brought in to look into Matt's death confidentially. And they were asked to give you their full cooperation."

"Great. Let's get started," I said, rising.

We walked toward the dressing room area. "Are the judges here?"

She shook her head. "They're rarely around until it's showtime."

"How about Mitch Reynolds? Or Ian Braithwait?"

"Mitch has been around a lot lately because of the...uh, situation. Usually not so much. He's responsible for half of prime time. And Ian rarely leaves his office. He only comes over here for the last two or three shows of the season."

"So who do you work for?"

"Tootsi Frootsi Productions. Mitch is network. Tootsi was originally Ian's baby. But after *Star Maker* became such a big hit, Rodney leveraged his way into joining him as executive producer."

I was about to ask how he had finessed that when I heard the sound of a woman furiously screaming. I ran down the corridor, concerned that someone was being attacked.

I was right, but not in the way I thought. Heads were popping out of doorways to find out what the commotion was about. The screaming was coming from the third doorway on my right. I ran into the room, which was brightly lit, with a long vanity mirror along one wall.

Down on the carpet, a girl with short spiky magenta-tinted hair, dressed in blue jeans and a T-shirt, was on her back, fighting for her life. "You bitch," she screamed. She continued to yowl wordlessly as she bucked and clawed.

I was surprised she could make any noise, because, sitting on her chest, trying quietly and with great determination to choke the air out of her, was a large black girl with a towering hairdo dressed in a terrycloth robe that was falling open.

I had never broken up a fight between two women before and I hesitated for a moment. Roxie stepped past me.

"Ladies," she said loudly.

The two girls halted their wrestling match for a moment and looked over at us.

"If you don't mind," said Roxie sarcastically, "this is Jim McNamara, the detective hired by the show. Jim, this is Eva." She gestured at the girl on the floor: "And this is Shontika."

I opened my mouth to say something witty and conciliatory, but before I could get a word out, the two girls simultaneously resumed battling. Now both of them were caterwauling.

And even though they were both *Star Maker* finalists, I couldn't discern any harmony in their duet.

*U*ncomfortable with manhandling a woman, I held back. Fortunately, not everyone had that compunction. A bulky man in a tan turtleneck and new-looking jeans with rolled-up cuffs brushed past me and yanked Shontika up and off the other girl. I assumed he was security because he looked to me like the bouncer on *The Jerry Springer Show*, the one who was always breaking up brawls. But lumpier and with a worse haircut.

Shouting, "Whoa, whoa, whoa," a small and skinny black man with a sparse mustache and a rodent-like face skittered past on my other side and gave Eva a hand up to her feet. He was wearing a short-sleeve, cable-knit, see-through black shirt and baggy jeans that exposed most of his patterned boxers.

Eva made a show of charging at Shontika again, but young blood jumped in her path with his arms out. "Nah," he said. "We ain't havin' no more of that."

Making menacing gestures with her hands, Shontika was being gently but firmly carried out of the room by the security guy.

During their battle, I had noticed that Shontika never let up on her choke hold, while Eva, for her part, wasn't scratching at her opponent's eyes or trying to pull her hair, either of which she could have reached. It looked like the whole time she was trying to sink her nails into Shontika's throat. Interesting approach. Battle of the divas.

As Eva's handler sat her down and began to talk soothingly to her, Roxie and I, along with the other witnesses, dispersed into the corridor.

"Do you know what that was about?" I asked.

Roxie shrugged, her palms up, a twinkle in her eyes and a barely suppressed smile on her lips. A lot of girls would have been upset at the display of aggression, but I got the sense she was amused by the spectacle. I was beginning to like her.

The large peace-maker emerged from a dressing room down the hall and began walking toward us. Something about his appearance—maybe his blimpy size or the way you could see his skull through his buzz cut—made me think of Bazooka Joe's posse, the funky cartoon characters you found wrapped around your bubble gum.

"Nice job," I said.

"Thanks, I guess," he said, grinning crookedly.

"You have to break up the contestants often?"

He looked at me with puzzlement.

"Jim, this is Cletus Renfro," said Roxie. We shook hands. "He's one of the finalists. Cletus, this is Jim McNamara. He's looking into Matt's, uh, accident."

"I'm sorry," I said abashedly. "I thought you were security."

"Happens all the time," he said easily.

"Really?"

"Well, I don't mean here. But if I'm like in Kmart, people always come up to me and ask where they can find stuff. No matter where I go, people always think I work there."

"Have you picked your song yet, Clete?" asked Roxie, detouring us away from my embarrassment.

"Not yet. It's going slow today. I believe I'm up after Patsy."

"Can I ask you a couple of quick questions?" I inquired.

"Shoot."

"Did you know Matt well?"

The corners of his mouth tugged down as he considered this. "Not as well as some of the others. He hung out mostly with John. They both auditioned in Milwaukee and roomed together out here. But he seemed like a nice guy, not snobby or nothing. I was looking forward to getting to know Matt better when we all moved into the house together."

"Is John still here?"

Roxie shook her head. "He didn't make the cut," said Cletus.

"Did you notice any hostility between Matt and any of the other contestants?"

Cletus turned his head and looked at the ceiling as he pondered. He looked back at me as he answered. "Not really. Like I say, he didn't mix with us too much, but he seemed pretty easy-going."

"Where you from, Cletus?"

"Jonesboro, Arkansas. I auditioned in Memphis."

"Cool. Thanks."

He nodded. "All right, see you around."

As he walked back to the rehearsal space, Roxie turned to me. "What next, Cappy?"

"Cappy?"

"Short for captain. So?"

"Why don't we work our way down the corridor and you can introduce me to whatever contestants are around?"

She gestured with her hand. "Lead on, MacDuck."

I looked at her, intrigued. "Is that a Shakespearean pun?"

"Search me," she said, her mouth in a moue. "It's something my father says. Usually when he's taking kids into his office to suspend them."

"Great," I said, walking down the hall, glancing into each room.

First up on the right, the purple-haired tigress Eva was still being counseled by the little baggy-pantsed peacemaker. I retreated, convinced by the glower on Eva's face that this would not be a good time to connect.

Hooking a thumb at the doorway, I whispered to Roxie, "Who are they again?"

She glanced in past me and backed up. "The girl is Eva. Eva Dortch, she's a single mom from a small town in Texas. Guthrie, I think. The guy is Flip Carson. From St. Louis. Him and Clete are inseparable."

Across the hall, I could hear singing before I entered the room. A girl was standing in front of the mirror, doing some acrobatic vocal exercises, flying up and down the octaves. I have a pretty good voice, but I could no sooner repeat what she was doing than I could play "Flight of the Bumblebee" on the flugelhorn.

She saw us in the mirror and turned to greet us with a dimpled smile. "Hi, Patsy," said Roxie. "This is Jim McNamara. He's the independent investigator we talked about. Jim, this is Patsy Harris."

~nodded. She got up and walked over to shake hands.
~ to meet you," she said.

Patsy had lustrous, chestnut-colored hair that fell in layers down to her shoulders. I'm helpless when it comes to describing hairstyles, but I thought of it as a shag, if that helps. She had a cute-as-a-button Meg Ryan type of face, with eyes that startlingly matched her hair color. But there was an inescapable cast of sadness to them.

Looking at her, I thought of the Neil Young song, "Cinnamon Girl."

"How old are you, Patsy?"

"Seventeen."

I would have guessed fifteen. "I just wanted to say hello, maybe get your take on Matt."

The sad quality in her eyes deepened. "He was a great guy. I still can't believe it," she said, shaking her head. Her eyes began to puddle with water. "Sorry," she said, walking over to the vanity counter to grab a tissue.

"I'm sorry to intrude. I'll talk to you later," I said, retreating into Roxie. As we exited, Patsy called out to me, "Mr. McNamara?" I turned. She wiped her cheek. "Good luck. Please catch whoever did this."

I nodded and left.

Further progress convinced me that you can't tell the players without a program. In the next room, we found a guy reclining in a leather chair, his blunt-toed motorcycle boots propped up on the makeup counter as he talked on his cell phone. I was convinced he was a Teamster—maybe a dues enforcer.

He was rough trade, a young black man with the steely musculature of a Doberman on steroids. He had a head like an anvil, accentuated with a wedged fade. His hair looked like a tree growing sideways on a wind-blasted cliff above the ocean.

I started backing out of the room, but Roxie took hold of my bicep. So we stood there watching him talk for ten seconds until our continued scrutiny began to bother him.

"Hold on a second, LaTron," he said, cupping the phone in his big hands. Then he looked over at us with annoyance.

"Sorry to bother you, Greg," said Roxie with a weary tone that let him know she was anything but. "But I'm taking Jim McNamara around to meet all the finalists. Jim is looking into the situation with Matt. Jim, this is Greg Jeffers. Greg, Jim."

He looked me over and gave a quick tip of his shovel-shaped chin in greeting. I lifted a palm. "How's it going?" I asked.

He scowled and then returned to his call, spinning in his chair so his back was to us.

"Charming," I observed out in the hall.

"Yeah, well, he may look like a gangbanger, but he sings like an angel," said Roxie. "Greg is the guy who was brought back to replace Matt."

"Where's he from?"

"Somewhere in Florida. Belle Glade, I think?"

"Who's next?"

"Let's see," she said, sticking her head in across the hall, then walking into the room, gesturing with her hand for me to follow. Two girls, heavily made up, were fussing in front of the mirror. The one nearest us was a stunner with platinum hair, big blue eyes, epic cheekbones and sensuous lips. She looked like a blonder Cameron Diaz. "Ladies, this is Jim McNamara. He's the investigator you were told about. You're to give him your complete cooperation. Jim, ̇ ̇JoJo. JoJo Johnson."

̇ ̇ stopped teasing her eyelashes, swiveled in ̇ ̇ "Pleased to meetcha."

"And this is Robin Cracknell," continued Roxie, extending her hand toward the other girl, a darkly complected brunette with a pneumatic body and long hair that looked pressed. The eyeliner she was busily applying wasn't doing much for her sallow orbs.

"The name's Neveah," she said tartly. "N-E-V-E-A-H."

"Pardon?" said Roxie.

Her eyebrows tried to migrate to the top of her scalp. "My name isn't Robin. It's Neveah."

"Since when?"

"As of today," she said, peering closely at her reflection.

"Have you run this by the producers?"

She waggled her head and bobbled her eyes to indicate how remedial the question was. "Of course," she said. "Ian thinks it's cool. I suggest you get used to it." JoJo reached across and gave her mirror-mate's hand a reassuring pat.

"I'll do that... *Neveah*," said Roxie.

"I hope we can arrange to get together, maybe tomorrow, to discuss Matt," I said.

Without looking in our direction, they both gave dismissive waves as we left. They were already reabsorbed in the important work of self-beautification.

I could see Roxie was tweaked by the most recent encounter, but I didn't want to give her an opportunity to vent. "Anybody else?" I asked innocently.

She exhaled and strode down the corridor, quickly surveying the final three rooms. "Nope," she said, turning back to me. "Let's see... you saw Ricky out on the floor. That means you met everybody but Bobby."

"Bobby?"

"Bobby Turner. He's probably over in the executive offices hitting on one of the secretaries."

"Ladies' man?"

Roxie's eyes looked to the heavens for help. "The worst."

"I heard that," came a voice from behind us. Imagine Harpo Marx crossed with Denzel Washington. That's the guy who glided into the hallway, his hands held up innocently, an insinuating smile on his lips. He had a thatch of tightly curled hair and thick, sensuous features. His coloring was extraordinary, a gleaming ginger hue.

"Roxie, Roxie, Roxie," he said, shaking his head and advancing toward us. I glanced over at Roxie. Her face was flaring with embarrassment. "Just because I find you irresistible don't make me no Casanova."

"Bobby," she said, then cleared her throat, "this is Jim McNamara. Jim, Bobby Turner."

"Hey, how ya doin'?" he said, smiling and flicking his chin at me but making no attempt to shake hands. He was dressed head to foot in faded denim with white tooled cowboy boots. The hair and the heels added a good four inches to his stature.

"I hear I missed a big fight," he said. "Shontika against Eva? Shit, I'd take Shontika against anyone in this crew. That girl could kick Greg's ass."

"Fuck you, Bobby," shouted a voice from one of the dressing rooms. I assumed Shontika's. He chuckled.

"Where'd you come from, Bobby?" asked Roxie. "I didn't see you in there a few minutes ago."

"I was trying on some clothes in wardrobe," he said, hooking a thumb over his shoulder. "But you really ⸂ ⸃dn't talk about people behind their back, baby."

"⸂⸃u tight with Matt, Bobby?" I asked. He was ⸂⸃ie, savoring her discomfort. He snorted ⸂⸃ves from her.

"There's only room for one rooster

in the barnyard. Dude was jealous of me." Loud staccato bursts of derisive laughter rang out from several dressing rooms.

"Roosters also tend to fight if they're confined together," I said, regarding him. "You have that problem with Matt?"

"Me?" he said, hooking his chest with his thumbs. I thought for a second he was going to break out into a song from *Peter Pan*. "I'm a lover, not a fighter. Ask anyone." He winked at Roxie.

"Interesting.... Well, we'll see you around campus, Bobby," I said, touching Roxie's shoulder and gesturing down the hall. As we walked away, I glanced back. Bobby was leaning against the wall, watching Roxie's ass and smirking.

As we entered the rehearsal room, Roxie said to me, "Well, now you've met everyone. God help you."

Over by the piano, Cletus was huffing and puffing his way through "Working for a Livin'." The song sounded odd and incomplete with just a piano. I hoped the big guy learned to play the harmonica by the time of the telecast.

But there was probably a rule against *Star Maker* contestants using an actual instrument onstage. Showing any musical ability would give them an unfair advantage.

"So, Roxie," I asked when Cletus paused to confer with Sandy, "why did you keep introducing me with euphemisms? 'This is Jim. He's here to look into Matt's *situation*.'"

Her eyes widened. "Because, Mr. Discreet," she said, reaching over to pinch my wrist with her fingernails for emphasis, "there's a reporter in the house."

I scanned the peanut gallery. In the far corner, a guy with black Brillo hair and a whomping big forehead had buttonholed Patsy. She was smiling politely, but there was a trapped look to her eyes. The reporter, who looked like Napoleon Dynamite's dance instructor, had adopted a lawn jockey pose with one arm up like he was holding a lantern. Then I spotted the micro tape recorder in his hand.

"Who's he work for?"

"*USA Today.* His name's Dan Rubowski. He's the one we spoon-fed that story about Matt withdrawing from the show. The one that ran in today's paper. Because he did such a fine job of taking dictation, he's been rewarded with a week backstage."

Patsy was looking at the reporter like he was a bad dentist. I was willing to bet his all-access pass didn't extend to Mitch Reynolds and Ian Braithwait. They wouldn't submit to his inane questions, but they had no problem inflicting him on the kids.

I considered what sticking around for the rest of the afternoon would gain me. Judging from what I had heard so far, probably a bad headache.

"Could you drive me back to my hotel?" I asked Roxie.

"Sure," she said, leaping to her feet.

As we walked to the parking lot, I inventoried for her the things I would need right away. "I want to look at all the tape you can get me of Matt, from the audition rounds right up until his most recent appearance."

She nodded.

"And see if you can get me a contact for Matt's roommate, John. Oh, and I'll need to talk to the police officer who investigated his murder."

Roxie pressed her key console and a blocky gray and black Honda that looked like a Lego car jolted to life. Sitting in the front seat behind the outsized windshield, I felt like I was in the Pope-mobile. As we fastened our seat belts, I added, "At the first opportunity, I want to address the finalists as a group."

"What do you want to say to them?"

"I'm not sure. But I want to see the dynamics when they're together."

"Okay, I'll check the call sheet. Maybe tomorrow morning at the mansion," she said, backing out of her space.

"How about in the production company? Were any of the people you work with close to Matt?"

"I can't think of anyone offhand. I'll ask around."

"Is it weird working for Ian?"

"Not really," she said, looking at me skeptically. "Why do you ask?"

"Because the guy's such a lush. How does a guy that far gone run a successful show?"

"Don't be fooled. Ian is plenty sharp. Each season, just after the finalists are picked, he's written down the name of the person he thinks will win and sealed it in an envelope. He opens and reads it at the wrap party. And every year he's been right."

When we pulled in at the hotel, there was a guy leaning against a parked Escalade just past the entrance. He was wearing a red beret that was puffed up on his head like a soufflé and rimless metallic light blue sunglasses. But I knew the expression on his face—like a cat that has been living on a steady diet of canaries.

"Whitey?" I called out as I opened the door.

He grinned, a smile so warm it could toast bread. "Hey, Jim!"

We walked toward each other and hugged. Curious thing about Whitey. Maybe it was his affable, teddy-bear manner, but he always seemed smaller and softer than he actually was. I only realized his real size on those rare occasions when we embraced and I suddenly felt like Jimmy Olsen. Then I promptly forgot it again.

"Hardly recognized you," I said.

"Same old me," he said, holding his hands at his sides in mock protest.

"Except you pimped your ride something fierce," I said, gesturing at the Cadillac SUV. "What happened to the old convertible? You trade up?"

"It's a loaner," he said sheepishly. "Hell, that ain't exactly right. When you bring a '74 Olds into the shop, they don't give you a loaner. But one of my sponsees has a business putting custom rims on these bad boys. He's busier than a sign-language translator at a Robin Williams concert. He's letting me drive this monstrosity until the old gunboat is fixed."

"And what's with the hat? You look like Rerun on *What's Happening!*"

"You don't like it?" he asked, touching his head self-consciously. "I'm trying to set a new trend."

"I think it looks very smart," said Roxie. She had parked the car and was walking toward us.

"Roxie, this is Whitey. Whitey, Roxie." They smiled at each other and shook hands.

"Roxie works for the people who hired me. Whitey is an old friend." It was a way of getting around saying we were in the AA program together.

"You work for Fox?" Whitey asked Roxie.

"No, Tootsi Frootsi."

"Really?" he said. "You know Joanie Hayden?"

"I *love* Joanie," she said. "She is such a sweetheart." And they were off and chattering away.

It didn't surprise me in the least that Whitey knew of my arrival and who had hired me. If a traffic light went out on Wilshire Boulevard, he heard about it. When it came to Los Angeles, the guy was damn near omniscient.

"Uh, guys," I said a minute or two into their trading of acquaintances. "Could we move this inside?"

"Wow," said Roxie, stopping to look around once we

were in the lobby. "Your hotel looks like Tammy Wynette's dollhouse."

It was only twenty yards over to the elevators, but in that space a couple of people shook hands with or called out to Whitey.

"Okay," said Roxie, halting in the corridor outside my room, "so I'll get together whatever tape I can of Matt in the audition rounds. Are you guys going to be here?"

Whitey and I looked at each other. "Yeah, for the most part," I said. "We may go out for an hour or so."

"Do *you* have a cell phone, Whitey?" she asked.

"Of course," he said, reaching in his pocket and handing her a card.

She glanced at it, then smirked at me. "Does it give you some kind of perverse pleasure to be the only man in America without a cell?"

I walked into my room without answering. Frankly the topic bored me and I didn't feel like explaining for the umpteenth time my aversion to this noxious and ubiquitous bit of modern technology.

If I were a parent with teenagers I might consider carrying a cell. But I'm more than a decade and a stable relationship removed from that situation. So I see no need to be in constant touch with the rest of the world. I don't share the sense of urgency. And carrying one of those devices makes me feel like a lab rat hooked up for periodic electric shocks.

Whitey and Roxie kept chatting in the hall. I went into the bathroom and washed my hands. I notice I've been doing this fairly regularly—for instance, after my mother calls. Washing my hands has become for me the punctuation to conversations I don't feel like having. Maybe I'm developing a Pontius Pilate complex.

On the plus side, I haven't come down with a cold in five months.

When I emerged, Roxie had left and Whitey had come in and closed the door.

"She's really nice, don't you think?" Whitey asked.

"You have a business card?" I countered incredulously.

"You're changing the topic. That means you like her."

I glanced at my hands, deciding it was too soon to wash them again.

CHAPTER
10

I settled into the room's overstuffed armchair. Whitey was looking out my window, which faced the back of the building. "Just in terms of staying true to the motif, shouldn't this hotel have a big cornfield out back instead of a swimming pool?"

"This is Los Angeles, bubba. You have to make certain concessions. Besides, that's not a swimming pool; it's a ce-ment pond."

He was distractedly twisting the curtain strings. "So Matt Hanes is dead and it's our job to find out who killed him. Is that about the shape of it, Kemo Sabe?"

I nodded. "What have you heard?" I asked.

"Drugged and then smothered."

"Not according to *USA Today*. Matt Hanes is still alive and has left the show for personal reasons."

Whitey snorted. "I don't believe anything I read in the

entertainment section of *USA Today*. It's not a newspaper; it's a message board for publicists."

"All right, let's go with drugged and smothered."

"You realize Matt's death changes everything," Whitey said, throwing himself in the room's other chair. The wicker screamed in protest. "He was the overwhelming favorite. A lock. The rest of that field are dogs. Now it's anybody's show to win."

"I just met them for the first time. But if you're going on looks, the blond girl, JoJo, is a stunner."

"Yeah, and my cat sings better than she does. No chance. That's the problem with this season. The ones who can sing, like Cletus and Greg, ain't winning no beauty contests. And the ones who are good-looking, like JoJo, sing like Roseanne. Matt was the only one with the whole package."

"That young kid Patsy seems to have a good voice."

He shrugged. "She'll probably make it to the final three. But that little sister vibe she's got never wins *Star Maker*."

"So who's that leave?"

"Nobody, really. I mean, Ricky will probably stick around till the end because the girls who dominate the voting always seem to develop a crush on the guy contestant who's the gayest. Right now, I'd probably pick Bobby Turner, but only if he learns to fake a little humility on air. He wouldn't have stood a chance if Matt was still around."

"You're freaking me out, Whitey. I can't believe how much thought you've given to who might win *Star Maker*."

"Are you kidding? You know this is a big gambling town. And I like to have tips to pass along to people. It's the equivalent of handing out cigarettes in a prison yard. When I heard we were going to be working backstage at *Star Maker*, I flipped. For me, that's like winning the lottery. "

"Wait a minute. You mean people bet on *Star Maker*?"

"Hello! It's bigger than the freakin' Super Bowl. Vegas has already posted lines on the eventual winner. Of course, the primary wagering is on who will get eliminated each Wednesday. But you can bet on every aspect of the show. Hell, there are bookies who will even take bets on what body part Sugar will have bandaged up that week."

Sugar Kane was the female judge, always sitting between Rodney and L. A. Cooper and always finding something to compliment about every performance.

"It's insane the money that gets bet on this show," Whitey continued. "And Matt's death throws everything up in the air. He was the three-to-one favorite."

"Huh. So it's possible somebody saw killing Matt as a way to improve their odds."

"Are you kidding? That's the first thing I thought."

"I'm not sure what you mean about Sugar's bandages." Ms. Kane's face was everywhere—she was a special correspondent on *Entertainment Tonight* and had even hosted *Saturday Night Live* a few months before. But I paid her no attention. She was one of those annoyingly vapid and ubiquitous personalities who seem to be cropping up all over the place in the Paris Hilton era.

In fact, until Whitey mentioned it, I had even spaced on her name. The thing is, Sugar had barely qualified as a celebrity during her period of maximum fame. And that was a long, long time ago.

Sugar had been a dancer on some dreadful TV music show. Don't hold me to this, but I think it was *Solid Gold*. Somehow that led to a record contract.

She became a one-hit wonder in the early eighties with "Tony." I consider myself strong on pop trivia, but even I have trouble dredging up that tune. Maybe that's a sign that it's better left forgotten.

A rock magazine recently named Starship's "We Built This City" the worst song ever recorded. Ha! "Tony" makes "We Built This City" sound like "Unchained Melody."

It was a strident and tinny earache with a chanted chorus that sounded like it was taken from a high school pep rally. But that kept Sugar from having to do any actual singing. And the video, with Sugar and a group of aspiring porn stars leaping around in pigtails and skimpy cheerleader outfits, was enough to put "Tony" on top of the charts for one long dreadful autumn.

Sugar tried to capitalize on her brush with fame. She married one of the Coreys (I don't recall if it was Feldman or Haim)—a union that lasted as long as one of J. Lo's. And she put out an exercise video. This was back in the era when this sweaty genre was like minting money. Keith Richards could have put out an aerobic tape and it would have gone platinum. You can almost see him, can't you? Raspily counting off leg lifts in a leotard and headband, a cigarette dangling from his lip.

Only Sugar's video failed. Maybe it was the persistent rumors that she was shot with an elongating lens to make her appear thinner. She promptly dropped off the zeitgeist radar, only to be revived somewhat eerily two decades later by *Star Maker*.

"What bandages?"

"You really don't watch the show, do you?" Whitey asked with unmistakable amazement. He shook his head. "Okay, I guess it started a couple of seasons ago, but Sugar started showing up each week with a different part of her body damaged. At first everyone thought it was some kind

of weird fashion statement. Like Nelly. But then she grad-
uated to splints and casts."

Whitey started chuckling. "One week...one week she
showed up with her head bandaged, like maybe she had
brain surgery. She looked like one of those amnesiacs on
a soap opera. And she always favors the spot that's bandaged, touching it and wincing a lot when the camera's on
her. So everyone will know she's really hurting.

"I don't know if she's hypochondriac or if she has—
what do you call it—Baron Munchhausen syndrome."

"Bizarre. So remind me again. What's the deal with the
other judge?"

He looked at me askance. "Maybe I should handle this
case. You can be second chair."

"It wasn't the judges who got killed. It was one of the
contestants. And I think I'm qualified to handle that."

"I'm not so sure," said Whitey. "You may be the only
guy in this country under the age of seventy who doesn't
know L. A. Cooper's name."

I sincerely doubted that. Cooper, a burly and officious
black man, was completely unknown before *Star Maker*.
And I had no doubt he would reenlist in obscurity as soon
as the show went off the air.

The thing I remembered about him from the period when
I checked out the show for a few weeks was that he was a
terrible name-dropper. He would preface most of his on-air
comments with boasts like, "When I was in the studio with
U2..." or "You know I worked with Mariah and..."

It tweaked me that this guy could have been such a
ubiquitous figure in the business and still be so completely
unfamiliar to me. So I went back through the credits of
the artists he mentioned, and never found his name listed
in any function. As far as I know, no one ever called him
on this.

"You want to hit a meeting?" Whitey asked. "I know one right down the street that starts in thirteen minutes." He wasn't looking at a clock. Whitey always seemed to know the exact time, although I never saw him consult a watch. Maybe he was digital.

"Sure."

As we left the hotel, it occurred to me I hadn't asked Whitey to work with me. He had just insinuated his way onto the case. That was fine, since I had intended to call him anyway. But something else struck me.

"Hey, Whitey?"

"Yeah, boss?"

"I'm just curious. How is it that you knew I was here, who hired me and where I was staying?"

He shrugged. "Dumb luck. A guy from my home group, Paul, is one of the receptionists at Television City. He overheard you talking to the guy next to him and then he saw you wandering off with your bags like a refugee.

"He called me up and said, 'Isn't this McNamara the guy who helped you recover Trent Reznor's master tapes?'"

I ignored the way our roles had been reversed. Instead I asked, "You talk about me at AA meetings?"

"Don't flatter yourself, Eek-a-Mouse. I was bragging about my incredible detective prowess to Paul and a couple of other guys at a picnic. So he calls and says, 'You better help your boy. He just wandered out the gates at TV City looking like a guy in dire need of a red cap.' I figured if you were on foot, there were only a few options. My second call was to a desk clerk I know at the Farmer's Daughter. Mission accomplished."

"Small world," I observed.

"Yeah, but I wouldn't want to mop it," Whitey said.

We walked over to a dilapidated bungalow set in a courtyard on West Third Street. It was a topic-discussion meeting. The speaker, seated at a brightly lit table at the front of the room, talked about change. When he turned it over to the crowded flock facing him in folding chairs, many hands went up, hoping to be called on. They looked like the White House press corps trying to get the President's attention.

"Gloria," the speaker said, pointing to a middle-aged woman with a ponytail and a weather-creased face in the front row. She waited until a microphone was passed to her to say, "I'm Gloria and I'm an alcoholic."

"Hi, Gloria," chorused the room.

I've seen microphones at meetings before, but usually it's in big rooms with bad acoustics. This was a rather cozy setting.

Before she continued, Gloria looked up and over her shoulder expectantly. Suddenly the light that had been focused on the speaker shifted over to her. Satisfied, she began to share.

Stunned at this turn of events, I turned to look up. There was a narrow rafter running under the eave of the building, with a slight elderly man leaning on the railing next to an adjustable floodlight.

I looked at Whitey in disbelief, leaning in to whisper to him, "They have spotlights at this meeting? And microphones?"

He smiled and, without looking at me, whispered out of the corner of his mouth, "This is L.A., bubba. You have to make certain concessions."

CHAPTER 11

Back in my hotel room, we hadn't even sat down when the phone rang.

"Hello?"

"Korean or Mexican?"

"What?"

"It's Roxie. I was bringing over the tapes and I thought I'd...unless you guys have already eaten."

I was pretty lost. "No, but..."

Whitey called to me, "Is that Roxie?" I nodded.

He walked toward me with his hand out. "Let me talk to her."

At the same time, in my ear Roxie said, "Put Whitey on the phone."

I happily withdrew, walking over to my computer to check my e-mail.

"Korean," said Whitey decisively. I discovered that question is a common cuisine choice in southern California. I don't even want to tell you where my mind took it, but it wasn't food. In my neck of the woods in Connecticut, the takeout choices are pretty prosaic: pizza or Value Meal.

"No, he's not always like this," said Whitey, chuckling. He glanced at me and then turned his back to talk in a quieter voice. The kids were making friends. Nice.

I checked my in-box. Same old. I hope everyone is getting bombarded with remedies for erectile dysfunction and that they haven't discovered some telltale sign in my consumer profile that indicates I might be especially interested. I was stripping out the day's bumper crop of offers for a simple blue pill when Whitey hung up.

"How'd you know it was Roxie?" I asked.

"Because you got all flustered."

Great. Now we were back in junior high. I was rescued from what had all the makings of a home room conversation by a message from *SylHanes@aol.com*. The subject field read, *Personal & Confidential*. I opened the e-mail.

Dear Mr. McNamara,

I am the mother of Matthew Hanes. I hope you don't mind my contacting you. I was given your e-mail address by Mr. Reynolds's office.

I know you must think we are terrible parents, leaving on a cruise just days after burying our son. But it's important to me that you know my husband, Arthur, and I were devastated by Matthew's death. He was our only son and he meant the world to us. I haven't stopped crying since we were notified. I am crying now.

The only reason we agreed to go on this cruise— and believe me, we are not fit company for the Lido deck; we mostly sit in our cabin and weep—is that

Mr. Reynolds and his lawyer assured us that we would be a hindrance if we stayed around. Particularly if we came out to Los Angeles, which is what we wanted to do. But they told us you could do your job better and faster if we didn't interfere.

I know this letter probably constitutes meddling, but I can't help it. I had to write.

Please. A grieving mother begs you. Please find my son's murderer. I would appreciate your letting us know of any developments.

God be with you.

Sincerely,
Sylvia Hanes

Great. No pressure.

I know the cases I write about usually involve murder, but homicide is involved in only a small percentage of the cases for which I'm hired. And those are my least favorite jobs, in part because of the added scrutiny of people like Matthew's mother. There are always loved ones hovering around, pointedly reminding you how much they're relying on you to find the person or persons responsible.

The thing is, I've done this enough to know that there is no satisfying the survivors. Not really. If I fail to find the culprit, they're bitterly disappointed and inform me in no uncertain terms that I've let them down. And you thought your job evaluation was harsh.

When I do find the killer, it still doesn't bring them peace. They think an arrest and conviction will make them feel avenged. It doesn't work.

In my experience, the only folks who come away from the murder of someone they care deeply about without severe and permanent scarring are the ones who somehow find their way to forgiveness. And I can't help them with that.

Reading the message from Mrs. Hanes, I also realized that Mitch Reynolds must have assured her that I was on the case before he had even hired me. Maybe I should have held out for four times my usual rate.

I sent a brief reply, expressing my sorrow for the family's loss and assuring them I would do my best.

Fifteen minutes later, I was getting my first glimpse of the victim, as Roxie, Whitey and I sat in my room watching *Star Maker* tapes while eating Mandu and Bi Bim Bap out of white cardboard containers.

My exposure to *Star Maker* had been pretty random and I had never tuned in early enough in the season to witness the audition process. Roxie told me it had become a popular part of the show, allowing the network to squeeze three additional weeks out of the series each year.

It was an astounding testament to the human capacity for delusion, an endless procession of the sorriest singers you've ever heard, all of them convinced they are the next Christina Aguilera or Josh Groban.

Imagine a dance contest in AP math class.

These singers, at least the ones they showed, weren't just bad. They were atrocious. How could they possibly imagine they stood a chance? It simply wasn't possible that any of these kids had ever received encouragement to perform. These were voices not even a mother could love.

Yet here they were, eager to show the world. It's one thing to think you don't sound bad when you're standing in the shower. But to stand in line for four days to make an utter fool of yourself on national television, that takes some powerful conceit.

I'm not sure exactly what to blame it on, but we seem to have raised a generation of kids who are convinced that they can all be stars, that underneath their ordinary exteriors is a vast storehouse of charisma and talent, heretofore untapped, which will somehow emerge if only they get a chance in front of a camera.

We're living in a fantasy nation, where despite all the evidence to the contrary, it's enough to believe in yourself, because confidence alone will transform you. *Star Maker* is both the apotheosis and the ultimate refutation of that magical thinking.

In this grotesque procession of tone-deaf freaks, Matt Hanes really stood out. No question about it: The kid could sing. That was obvious from the first time he stepped in front of Rodney, Sugar and L.A. in Milwaukee.

He had a smooth and burnished voice, the aural equivalent of a mahogany cabinet. It was a little on the old-fashioned side, like a really good lounge singer from the sixties. But he had terrific range, with a fairly sophisticated sense of dynamics and phrasing.

Good-looking too. Matt was strong and athletic, with lustrous, golden hair framing a broad face with handsome features and a ridiculously radiant, easy smile.

To my eye, he didn't resemble a singer as much as he did a tennis pro at a country club, or the rowing captain at some Ivy League university. He didn't look seedy enough for showbiz.

But there was no question he was a natural performer—easy, confident, charming. He flew through the early rounds, alternating "Build Me Up Buttercup" and "Since I Fell for You." From the start, he instinctively targeted Sugar, standing right in front of her as he performed, gesturing toward her when the lyrics were intimate, giving her his cocky "We have a little secret, don't we, baby?" smile.

She just lapped it up. It was embarrassing, really. She'd start to blush and her eyes would sparkle as soon as Matt walked in the room. Before he'd even open his mouth, she'd start fanning herself. By the time he was finished singing, they had to practically sponge her out of her chair.

But then, all the judges loved him. He was a refreshing note of quality amid a sea of vocal deformities. Even Rodney was enthusiastic about him—at least initially. The Brit's comments grew more acerbic with each round, which I ascribed to his well-documented orneriness.

Because certainly there was very little to criticize about Matt. When the competition moved to Los Angeles and onto a soundstage, his superiority to the rest of the pack was still obvious. His performances were flawless and he always seemed to know what camera was on him and to play directly to it. His banter with the judges was always relaxed and respectful.

No wonder he was the odds-on favorite to win. It was like seeing Jim Brown at the top of his game playing football with a bunch of Pee-Wee Leaguers.

If nothing else, the long tape session with Roxie and Whitey established motive. If I had to compete with Matt Hanes, I'd want to kill him myself.

CHAPTER
12

The next morning, Roxie picked me up in her Lego car and drove me out to the *Star Maker* house, a glassy and gaudy modern monstrosity set in a canyon high above the city. I suppose the view would have been impressive if only you weren't looking out over Los Angeles, which was like peering into a fishbowl that hadn't been cleaned in several weeks. But for the young finalists on *Star Maker*, it was a domestic Disneyland.

"Is this hard for you, coming out here?" Roxie asked solicitously as she navigated the twisty ascent.

"Hmm?" I kazooed absently, looking out the passenger window. Roxie was wearing a short navy skirt and I was trying to avoid looking at the way the muscles in her legs glided beneath her tan skin as she shifted adroitly through the gears. Instead, I was staring out at the scenery. Fighting another losing battle with my instincts.

"Whitey told me you got hurt pretty bad out in the Hollywood Hills."

"Yeah," I acknowledged, eyes right.

A few years ago, before I knew Whitey, I had been retained by a frantic record company owner whose early adaptation of rap had made him ridiculously wealthy. Then his fourteen-year-old daughter disappeared on a trip to the Sherman Galleria.

No ransom demands, just a muffled message on his cell cautioning him that if he brought in the police or the FBI, he'd never see Chloe again. As soon as he called me, I advised him to ignore the warning and contact the authorities, but he begged me to pursue it solo.

Because of the cell phone warning—a random perv couldn't get access to the number—I immediately started sifting through the label owner and his wife's wide social circle, narrowing it down to a small unsavory nucleus that included a sleazy sometime producer and, as I discovered, amateur pornographer. I paid an unannounced visit to the guy's expansive villa in the hills and found Chloe in his bedroom studio, drugged and dazed.

The creep caught up to us right outside the front door as I was walking her out to my car. Sneaking up behind me, he stuck most of a four-inch blade in my side. The surgeon who worked on me later told me I was extremely lucky because it missed my liver by millimeters.

As I crumpled to the ground, I told the girl to run, and thankfully she shuffled off, the slope of the driveway giving her momentum.

I grabbed the freak's ankle as he ran after her, giving Chloe a little more of a head start. When he broke free and chased her, I crawled back into the foyer and used his phone to dial 911 before passing out.

I never wrote about the case. It didn't seem real promising as a narrative—no celebrities, no murder involved and it was over in a hurry. On the other hand, I did lose a lot of blood, if that counts for anything. But all I have to show for it is a small welt of raised pink skin on my side. I've seen people come out of appendicitis operations with more scar tissue.

I rarely think about the incident, except when the weather conditions conspire to give me a nasty visceral twinge. And I wasn't thinking about it now. I never do out here. Los Angeles doesn't have weather.

"I couldn't do what you do," said Chloe.

"It's not that dangerous, really. I could count the number of times I've been seriously maimed on the stubs of one hand."

"That's not what I mean. I wouldn't want to be suspicious of everyone, always questioning if people are lying to me. I'd rather take people at face value and be occasionally disappointed than doubt everyone."

"I'm probably less cynical about human nature now than I was when I started doing this job," I said sincerely.

"Wow," she said, opening her eyes wide in surprise.

"I don't assume everyone is lying to me—only the ones who have something to hide. And I think it was the Beatles who said, 'Everyone has got something to hide, 'cept for me and my monkey.'"

I looked over at her profile. She was smiling. That was good. She had passed the test. Girls who don't get Beatle references are too young for me to have a relationship with. Knowledge of Ringo, of course, is optional.

"Mostly what I do is go around asking questions, watching people's reactions and listening carefully to what they say...and what they don't say," I continued. "Speaking of which, I need your take on this too. Who do you think killed Matt?"

"I have no idea," she said, her voice flustered. "Believe me, if I had a strong suspicion I would have volunteered it."

"I'm sure you would have, Roxie. I wish it was easy enough that I could just walk in the room and someone would point and say, 'Joey did it.' Then we could all go home. You may not know who the guilty party is, but I'll bet you know a lot more than you realize. You've spent a lot of time around this group. I want your impressions, your take on these kids."

"So you're assuming it's one of the finalists?" she asked, looking at me with concern.

"At least initially, yeah. Drugging his pizza, that suggests to me someone very familiar with Matt's habits . . . unless you think it was someone from the production side?"

She considered the possibility for a moment and then shook her head. "I don't think so. Everyone was real glad we found Matt this year. It makes everyone's job easier. The talent has been pretty thin some seasons. And Matt seemed like the show's biggest slam dunk since Terry was on."

Even I knew Terry Taylor. He was the only winner whose fame transcended *Star Maker* (although I wasn't quite sure why). He was a geeky kid who resembled the Scarecrow from *The Wizard of Oz*. Then he opened his mouth and this gloriously sweet tenor poured out.

Shazam, as Gomer Pyle used to say.

The voice alone wouldn't have been enough to overcome Terry's carnival appearance. Even after his dramatic serial makeovers, Terry still looked like a neglected stuffed doll at a yard sale. But he had this soft-spoken Southern manner and freakishly long eyelashes that women—especially older women—seemed to respond to.

His popularity eclipsed all the other *Star Maker* winners. Platinum record sales, soft drink endorsements, network concert specials, even hosting gigs on superfluous awards shows—Terry had it all. Critics were calling him the next Barry Manilow, like that was a good thing.

"Besides," Roxie continued, "everyone seemed to genuinely like Matt." She pulled onto the curving driveway that led up to the *Star Maker* glass house. Two guys stood in our path, looking as comfortable in their ties and jackets as Herman Munster in formal wear. We held IDs up to Roxie's panoramic windshield and they stepped aside, waving us on.

"So give me your quick impressions before we go in," I said, as she parked in a paved oval just below the house.

"I guess Greg Jeffers is the obvious suspect, because he needed someone gone to get in the finals," she said, unsnapping her seat belt and turning to face me, her right calf coming up on the seat. "And while I don't like Greg—he's unbelievably rude—I think that's a defense. Even though he looks hard and mean, I don't think that he would kill someone, okay?"

I shrugged. I wasn't convinced of Greg's inner kindness.

"As for the rest, there's a lot of people in this crew that I don't trust—Eva, Flip, Bobby and Robin...oops," she said, holding up an index finger, "I mean *Neveah*...but again, killers?" She leaned over and glanced up toward the house. Then she sat back. "Having said that, if there's one thing I've learned working on this show, it's that the contestants—and this group more than most—will do anything, and I mean *anything*, to win."

I nodded and we got out. As we walked up the wide terraced steps toward the front entrance, I said, "I need you to be an extra set of eyes while we're in here. Pay attention to their reactions."

"I'm no detective," she objected.

"I know, but I think you're really sharp, Roxie. I need your help here."

She cocked her eyes, pleased at the compliment.

Inside, most of the kids were already gathered in the living room. It was an enormous space with high ceilings. The centerpiece was a riverstone fireplace, facing a long oval of a couch built into the sunken area in front of the hearth. A black Yamaha grand piano sat on the upper level, near the curving stairway leading up to the second floor. There was a large dining room that you stepped down to off to the left. Every floor surface I could see was covered with gaudy yellow shag carpeting.

I felt like I was in the Brady Bunch ski lodge.

Most of the girls, along with Ricky, were scattered along the wraparound couch, chatting and laughing. The stereo, set to a noisome Top 40 station, was blaring an Usher song. Cletus came in from the kitchen, trailed by Flip, both of them holding plates.

The big guy saw me and Roxie and gave us a friendly head bob, the only acknowledgment we had received from anyone in the room. He walked over to the stereo, turned the volume all the way down and shouted, "House meeting!" drawing the words out in a way that made me think of a hog call.

Thank you, I mouthed to Cletus. He smiled and settled into a place on the couch, Flip flopping down right next to him. Because of the difference in their sizes, they reminded me of an elephant with one of those birds riding on its shoulder. The elephant puts up with it because the bird grooms it. I wondered what Cletus got out of the arrangement.

A moment later Eva came down the stairs. Her spiky magenta hair was a mess, but I suppose that was the idea.

With her was Neveah. I had the same thought about the brunette that I had had when I'd first met her the previous day backstage at the Larry Hagman Theater: Nice body, nasty-ass personality.

Both of the girls were wearing surly frowns. They looked like a pair of bomb-throwing anarchists who had been interrupted right in the middle of conspiring.

Greg was next, his body English fluent with hostility. Without looking at anyone in the room, he came down and stood against the far left side of the fireplace, wearing earbuds from a small MP3 player tucked in his shirt.

See no people, hear no people, speak to no people.

Finally, preceded by loud laughter, Bobby appeared on the top landing with a dyed, sloe-eyed insta-blonde wearing last night's party dress and last night's makeup. He paused, making sure everyone was watching his entrance. I couldn't get over his complexion. Buff him a little bit and you could put him up on the mantel as an Oscar.

Bobby said something under his breath to the blonde. She laughed and gave him a familiar swat on the arm. His manner changed at the bottom of the stairs, as if some imaginary director had called, *Cut!*

"See you later, okay," Bobby said brusquely, patting his date's ass while also shoving her toward the door. "I got some show business to attend to." He walked over to the couch and started flirting with JoJo.

The peroxide party girl looked confused for a second, then angry. She glared at Bobby and opened her mouth to say something, then walked to the door, her gait stiff with insult.

I took up a position right in front of the fireplace to address them. Roxie stood off to my left, across from Greg.

"I know you have very hectic schedules," I said, "and I appreciate your making time for me. My name, once

again, is Jim McNamara. I believe you're all aware that I
have been brought here to look into Matt's death.

"No one spent more time with him over the last few
weeks than the people in this room. So I need your help. If
you have any theories or suspicions, any information at all
that might prove significant, I want to hear it."

Silence. It was so quiet I could hear the music playing
inside Greg's head. Thick skulls make for good acoustics.

JoJo was intently studying her fingernails; Greg was
staring at the floor; Bobby was playing footsie with
Neveah. The only people in the room looking at me were
Cletus and Patsy.

I felt like a substitute teacher in front of a high school
classroom.

"Okay," I said, pronouncing the word like a doorbell
chime to dispel the awkward silence. "I can understand
why you all are reluctant to talk, since the people in this
room are the primary suspects in Matt's murder."

That brought up a few heads. But not as many as you
might think.

I tried another tack. "Let's start with who was the last to
see him on the night he died."

Neveah raised a hand. "Yes, Neveah," I said.

"Umm, that would be Shontika," she said, all innocence.

Shontika stopped braiding strands of her hair long
enough to shoot Neveah a murderous glare. It was returned
with a triumphant smile.

"So what?" Shontika said, loud and belligerent. "That
don't prove shit. It's only because I had to pass Matt's room
on the way to the elevator. I stuck my head in and asked if
he was coming out with us. Doesn't mean I was the last to
see him. I'm just the only one willing to admit it."

That remark occasioned several covert glances around the room.

"You're right, Shontika," I assured her. "There's nothing suspicious about that." She rolled her shoulders in vindication. "So what did Matt say when you asked him?"

"Said, 'Nah,' he was gonna chill in his room."

"How did he seem to you?"

"Shit. I don't know. Normal? He smiled at me. He was always smiling."

I turned back to the group.

"And you went out to celebrate?" A few nods. "Where?"

A chorus rang out, "Bennigan's."

"Was everyone there?"

It got quiet. A few people looked at each other. Then Ricky spoke up. "Bobby wasn't there."

"Shut up, you little fag," Bobby said. There wasn't a lot of rancor in it. It was more of a knee-jerk insult. Bobby turned his head toward me. He wasn't looking at me, but in my general direction. "I didn't feel like eating potato skins. Big deal. I went to a club one of the crew told me about."

"Can anyone vouch for your whereabouts?" I asked.

"I met a girl," he said, unable to resist a self-satisfied smirk. I guess that sign of validation never got old for Bobby.

"You have her name and number?"

"I can probably come up with it," he said, shrugging.

"Make sure you do." I turned back to the group. "Everyone else together that night?"

"Yeah, well, except Greg," said Cletus. "He had already gone home and had to be flown back after...they found Matt." Greg looked up at me. Apparently he was hearing as much of the proceedings as he wanted to. I thought I detected a glimmer of vindication in his expression, but it was hard to tell through the bonfire of hostility. I considered asking him if he could verify his absence that night, but I knew what kind of reaction I'd get. Besides, that was something I could easily track down myself.

"All right, who spent the most time with Matt?"

"John," called out several voices. People are always most eager to blow the whistle on the guy who's not in the room.

I nodded. "Besides him," I said.

JoJo pointed a manicured finger at Patsy, who blushed a deep red. But I got the feeling she'd do that if she was singled out in any group.

"Did anyone here really not get along with Matt?"

Several quick looks darted around the couch, but no one spoke. I had seen two white vans pull up outside. As Roxie had informed me on the way up, it was time for the kids to tape this week's Ford commercial. I had already gotten as much out of them as I expected to, so I delivered my parting divide-and-conquer spiel.

"Thank you for your time. If there is anything you want to tell me that for whatever reason you weren't comfortable saying in front of everyone here, I would encourage you to seek me out. I'll be around every day."

As we started the drive down into the city, Roxie said, "Well, that was interesting."

"Yeah."

"I didn't get much of a reading from their reactions, did you?"

"Not really. But that's okay. I just came out here to shake their tree a little bit. See what falls out."

"Delayed reaction, huh?" she said, smiling.

"Sorta."

"I hope so," she said, "because they sure weren't volunteering much."

"No," I agreed. "I'd say they were thick as thieves."

I had been trying to reach the cop who had originally been assigned to Matt Hanes's murder. But Detective Mike Klingelhof wasn't returning my calls.

Par for the course. It's law enforcement's way of expressing their disdain for hired operatives like me. Let the fucker wait. A certain amount of ball-busting goes with the territory.

LAPD takes this passive-aggressive policy further than most jurisdictions. I guess the department's sterling reputation has earned them a certain hauteur.

Fortunately I had more success in contacting Matt's *Star Maker* roommate, John Drayton, in Racine, Wisconsin. His mother said he was working a split shift at Circuit City and she'd have him call me when he got home for lunch. Sure enough, the phone in my hotel room rang punctually at four-fifteen. Maybe I should try to find Detective Klingelhof's mother.

"Hi, this is John Drayton," he said, his voice relaxed and friendly. I'm used to catching a certain amount of attitude. "I'm trying to reach Jim McNamara."

"This is Jim. Thanks for getting back to me. I'm looking into Matt's death and I wanted to ask you a few questions."

"Sure. How's it going anyway?" he asked.

"Just getting started, really. You have any idea of who might have wanted to kill Matt?"

"Honestly, no. He was a super guy. I'm still in shock. But kill him? No."

"Did he have any conflicts with any of the other contestants?"

"Yeah, a few. A lot of that group that made it through to the finals are real pieces of work."

"Who'd Matt argue with?"

"I guess his biggest beef was with Flip." That didn't surprise me. The little guy who shadowed Cletus everywhere had a hustler vibe.

"Somebody stole some jewelry out of our room, and Matt was pretty sure it was him. He confronted him. They had a big shouting match in the hallway. Flip denied it, of course, and he accused Matt of being a racist, which was bullshit."

I could hear John's mom in the background, barking his name disapprovingly.

"Anyway, they didn't get along too well after that."

"Anyone else?"

"Let's see...he certainly had words with Eva on a few occasions."

No surprise there. The punky girl with the colors-not-found-in-nature hair seemed pretty antagonistic. The first time I had seen her, Shontika was trying to throttle her to death, and Shontika didn't seem like she rattled easily.

"What would Matt argue with Eva about?"

"Usually about how nasty she was. Everyone there was competitive, but Eva took it to a whole other level."

"How so?"

"Mostly playing head games with people. If a girl was insecure, Eva would remind her just before she sang of how much pressure was on her performance. The guys, she'd just insult. 'You really think you have a shot in this contest?' Stuff like that. One girl, Jessica, who was really talented, Eva took her out with a few other people the night before our final audition and really plied her with drinks. That's what I heard. Anyway, Jessie was a mess the next day. Rodney and the other judges were really disappointed. She was the female Matt."

"Wow," I said.

"That's not half of it. Eva is a capital-*B* bitch."

"John Randolph Drayton!" his mother remonstrated in the background.

"Sorry, Mom," he singsonged.

"Is there anyone else Matt tangled with?"

John huffed out an inventory-taking exhale. "Oh, Bobby. Matt didn't like him at all." There was a knock at my hotel room door.

"Hold on a sec, John," I said. "I have to answer the door." I opened to Whitey, still wearing the jaunty beret and glaring at me. He looked like a dyspeptic customs official in Marseilles.

"I can't believe you went out to the *Star Maker* house without me," he groused.

"Hold that thought," I said, holding up a finger. "I'm on the phone." I retreated to the table and picked up the handset. Still frowning, Whitey came in, shutting the door behind himself.

"I'm back," I said. "You were saying about Bobby?"

"Yeah, Matt went at it with him a lot."

"What about?"

"Patsy, mostly. Matt didn't like the way Bobby kept flirting with her."

"Jealous?"

"Unnnh, nah. I think it was more protective. He knew Bobby was just playing with her and he didn't want to see her get hurt. Patsy's a sweet kid and she was dealing with a lot already—her father suddenly popping up out of nowhere."

I was about to ask him to explain, but decided to just let him run his string.

"I mean, Patsy definitely had a crush on Matt. All the girls did, even one of the judges," John said, chuckling. "A lot of them hit on him. But Matt had a girlfriend at home. Anyway, in Patsy's case he was like a big brother to her. I don't think it went further than that."

"You ever meet Matt's girlfriend?"

"Nah. He showed me her picture a bunch of times and he talked to her on the phone at the same time every night. That's the reason he wouldn't go out and party with everyone else. He wanted to be in our room when Susan called.

"He wanted her to fly out if he made it to the top five, but that show has a lot of rules. One of which is no spouses or steadies shown on camera or mentioned in interviews. The audience is supposed to think everyone on that stage is available for dating."

I got the full name of Matt's girlfriend. John didn't have her number.

"Did Matt have any other conflicts, with one of the judges, maybe? Or the show's staff?"

"Not that I saw. He sure had Sugar eating out of his hand. But everyone connected with the show from the producers on down treated Matt special. He had the golden ticket. That's why I wanted to be his roomie. I figured maybe I could get through on his coattails."

"Well, how about people who had already been eliminated? Maybe someone jealous of how well Matt was doing?"

"You mean like me?"

"No, I wasn't thinking of you. But a lot of people were sent packing. Maybe one of them hung around."

"No one I can think of. I didn't see any real grudges against Matt."

I decided to throw him a bone. "You almost made it to the final round. That's pretty good, man."

"Yeah, well, I don't think I would have won the whole thing, but I should have made the finals. But Rodney had it in for me," he said, his voice turning bitter. "If it wasn't for him... After he said I had a voice like a duck with a ruptured spleen, I was finished. Asshole!"

I waited for the sound of John's mother to reprove him, but it never came. Either she had left the room or else she agreed with her son's assessment of Rodney.

"That's too bad," I said. "Look, thanks for your time. Before we get off, do you have any thoughts that might have bearing on Matt's death?"

"Huh." He thought for a moment. "Not really. I didn't see this coming at all. Not in the time I was there. I never felt like Matt was in danger. But I have to say, nothing that happens in Los Angeles could surprise me. That is one shady town. I don't know how anybody could live there."

"Me neither. Hey, before I let you go, someone told me you guys had pizza delivered every night."

"Yeah. We'd order a pie. Matt would have his conversation with Susan and then we'd watch *SportsCenter* while we ate."

"Was it the same delivery person every time?"

He paused for a second. "Gee, you got me. I never really noticed."

"Okay, thanks for your help, John."

"Sure. Good luck."

Whitey started in on me before the phone was even in its cradle. "I thought we were a team," he said.

"We are," I said with as much enthusiasm as I could muster. I've never been much of a team player.

"Then why would you interview all the primary suspects and not take me?"

"I didn't want them to feel overwhelmed. That's why I went out to their house. I hoped they wouldn't be as guarded on their own turf."

"Oh, right! Like I'm so intimidating," he said, throwing his hands out to the side in protest. He had a point. Standing there like that, he looked like Randy Quaid in a dinner theater production of the Marcelle Marceau story.

"It's not just that, Whitey. I want to hold you in reserve. They haven't seen us together and I'd like to keep it that way. That way as this goes along you can tail them and they won't know they're being observed."

This argument slowed his indignation.

Then I played my hole card, handing him the studio pass I had asked Roxie to get for him. Nothing like a laminated document to boost a man's spirits.

"That means when we go to tomorrow's taping, we enter separately and we sit apart."

"Right," he said, nodding, still studying his all-access card. Then he looked up at me. "So, you want to hit a meeting?" All was forgiven.

We had about forty-five minutes to kill, so we stopped at the Virgin Megastore on Sunset Boulevard. Walking up and down the aisles, I saw a display for a Mandy Moore greatest hits collection. There was a life-sized cardboard cutout of the singer. Amazing. A whole career founded on cheekbones.

Still, the greatest hits package struck me as presumptuous. Don't you have to actually have a hit before you can go that route?

Clearly, this was trend. There had been a big display as we walked in for Hillary Duff's *Most Wanted*. How the hell did she rate an anthology? She only had two exceedingly thin CDs under her belt. It was like a teenager writing an autobiography: *My Life so Far*.

One row over, there was a similar anthology devoted to Pearl Jam. It struck me, not for the first time, that I should switch my specialty, because rock music was clearly dying. Downloading wasn't the death knell. The industry had given up on finding new talent; all it cared about was repackaging its old inventory. And you can't last long once you start cannibalizing yourself.

Groups like Pearl Jam certainly hadn't helped matters, I thought as I frowned at the jewel case of *rearviewmirror*, looking in vain for a good song. Eddie Vedder was the Pandora of modern music, unleashing a raft of bad rock singers, a dreary army of murky baritones baring their tortured but brawny souls. I don't care how intense your feelings are, bud, they're no substitute for a good voice.

Everything is relative, though, right?

I was about to attend my first *Star Maker* show. After that, Eddie Vedder would sound like an angel.

Sometimes I wonder: Was I an asshole before I started abusing alcohol and drugs? Or did ten years of steadily soaking my brain in toxic chemicals turn me into one? Ultimately, it doesn't matter, I guess. The fact remains that I'm an asshole.

I've seen people undergo profound changes in AA. Complete transformations. That hasn't been the case with me.

Yeah, I haven't touched a drink or a mood-changing drug in nearly eight years, and believe me, that's a miracle. But left to my own warped devices, I'm still inherently dishonest, restless, angry and self-centered. What the program has given me is a desire to be the best person I can be. Most days I don't even get close to that ideal. But if I don't pray, meditate, go to meetings and try to work the 12 steps, I don't have a shot at all.

What I'm trying to say is that most of the time I'm

grateful to be sober and determined to stay that way. But not that next day. The thing is I truly love music. And hearing a batch of bad Huey Lewis songs mauled in a way that wouldn't pass muster at a middle school talent show was excruciating.

And the whole time, the crowd was stomping and cheering for this stale crap like they were at a U2 concert. Awful music, rapturously received—it created a dissonance in my head that was painful. Like the Ramones, I wanted to be sedated.

I walked to my torture session, because Whitey refused to pick me up. I was the one who suggested we pretend not to know each other at the theater. But it wasn't enough for Whitey that we walk inside separately. He didn't even want us to arrive at the gate in the same vehicle.

He was taking this whole spy-in-the-house-of-karaoke thing way too seriously, if you ask me. Whitey was in the building somewhere, I'm sure, but I never saw him. From my vantage with Roxie, just offstage behind the band riser, I could see the performers and the first few rows of the audience while keeping an eye on the TV monitor right in front of us.

The *Star Maker* performance show that aired on Tuesday night was taped on Monday—all day Monday. It was a simple formula, really. The host, an empty package of teeth, ego and frosted hair named Brian Breeze, would introduce the contestants one by one. Then there would be a break while they set up on the stage. A taped package about each of the finalists, shot during the audition process, would be inserted overnight.

Then they would sing. The crowd would go nuts. The judges would critique their outing. Breeze would get the kid's reaction and it was on to the next. But between Breeze's opening—"Welcome back, America. Your next

Star Maker champion is standing on this stage"—and his bizarrely inappropriate tagline—"Call me the Breeze"— yawned an eternity.

The thing is, every time Breeze muffed one of his spontaneous witticisms off the teleprompter (which was often), or the judges cursed at one another (same frequency), or the band hit a sour note (a couple of times per song), we started all over again in order to get a smoother take.

Only the kids were on their own. No do-overs. That was the idea anyway. JoJo was clever enough to figure a way around it. She looked smashing and surprisingly wholesome, an all-denim outfit setting off her shining blond hair. The makeup was more understated than what JoJo usually wore and there was a subtle spray of sparkles over the bridge of her nose and under her eyes. It looked like her fairy godmother had tapped JoJo's nose with a magic wand.

It was a fetching look for her, and on *Star Maker*, as I was to discover, how you looked was more important than how you sounded.

Anyway, when JoJo hit a particularly rough patch while warbling "Stuck with You," she simply substituted her own obscene lyrics. Breeze came running out onstage waving his arms to stop the take. (JoJo's strategy would be adopted by many of the other contestants in the following weeks during Monday tapings. Get in trouble? Start cursing.)

The multiple takes made the day stretch on forever. Throughout the long ordeal, the crowd had to be whipped up to a continuous froth, their frenzied reaction being a crucial component of the show. Four frighteningly energetic Tootsi Frootsi production assistants worked the aisles, egging on the audience. Those poor, constantly prodded people. All they got for their extraordinary effort was a Happy Meal and the type of singing that should have been covered by the Geneva Convention.

Flip, who was up first, set the tone for the evening. Smiling nervously and twisting from side to side with an agitated motion that reminded me of a washing machine, he sang "Hip to Be Square." His spangled shirt kept strobing out under the bright stage lights.

Because he was performing a song from long before his time, one which he probably had never heard, he enunciated the words stiffly. Flip and most of the singers who followed him sounded like they were Kurdish speakers, singing in English phonetically.

L. A. Cooper assailed him immediately. "Look at you! Look at you! How you feelin', yo?" A few people in the crowd chanted, "Coop, Coop." Flip smiled sickly, nodding his head. "Yeah, I don't know, duck," L.A. said, his chin up in the air. "I was in the studio with Huey, you know?" I assumed there was some point to this dubious assertion. There wasn't.

"This is the finals," he continued. "You got to bring your game way up. That didn't stoke me. Nah. Nah."

Breeze put a consoling arm around Flip, who didn't seem too upset at Coop's criticism. I'm not sure if he even heard it. Standing under the lights, pulled sideways by Breeze's grip, he looked shell-shocked. As the taping went along, I noticed that Breeze got close only to the shorter contestants like Flip, Eva and Ricky, convinced, I suppose, that it made him look tall. He treated the larger kids—Cletus, Bobby and Greg—like they were convent-school dance partners, keeping his distance at all times.

"You thrill me, Flip," said Sugar. Except with her breathy lisp it sounded more like: *You fwill me, Fwip.* "What a delightful note to start the competition on. And you have such a natural stage presence. Bravo."

Rodney stared at Sugar as if a nest of cobras were writhing atop her head. And I'm pretty sure it wasn't because she had just said "Bwavo." Turning back to the stage, he said wearily but distinctly, "That was an abomination. I've heard better voices at a cattle auction."

Something about his English accent made his insults sound even more sneering and dismissive.

As soon as Rodney started speaking, Sugar twisted around in her seat and started egging on the audience by jerking her thumb down as if she were hitchhiking to hell. The crowd responded by lustily booing Rodney. He smirked resignedly.

And we were off. Another thrilling season of *Star Maker*.

Neveah was up next. She wore a silver satin blouse that accentuated her breasts, which she brandished at the camera like Scud missiles. She also smiled a lot. While warbling a stiff version of "If This Is It."

"Yo, yo, how you feelin' babe?" L.A. wanted to know. "You started off kinda rough, a little sloppy there at the beginning. Ya feelin' me? But you brought it home in the end. It was aiight."

"What can I say, Neveah?" added Sugar. "You could charm the birds out of the trees. Nicely done."

Rodney shook his head. "Would you do me a favor, Neveah?" he asked. She stared at him with narrowed eyes, sensing the other boot was about to drop.

"When you go backstage, would you please inform the other contestants that this is a singing contest? Apparently someone forgot to tell you people. That was dreadful. Just dreadful." Boos rained down on him, which seemed to improve his posture.

The next singer, Ricky, got to do "I Want a New Drug," the song he had lobbied Sandy so abjectly for. We have a saying in the AA rooms: Be careful what you wish for. His monotonous singsong rendition wasn't only boring—it was distinctly painful.

I could have walked outside right then with a microphone, pulled five people at random off the line waiting for *The Price Is Right* taping, and all of them would have done as well as Ricky without rehearsal.

L. A. Cooper shook his head sadly. "Ricky, Ricky," he muttered. "What's going on, duck? I've heard you sing before, yo, so I know you got the flava. But not tonight. Nah, nah, not tonight."

Sugar stared at L.A. with dismay. Then she turned to the stage, smiling. "Ricky, your voice gives me goose bumps," she said, stroking her bare right arm, wincing as her hand reached her wrist, which was wrapped in a soft cast that wound around her thumb. "You have a beautiful instrument."

"Thank you, Sugar," said Ricky, fluttering his long eyelashes.

"How do you think you did, Ricky?" asked Rodney.

"Pretty good," said Ricky. Breeze gave the kid's shoulder an encouraging squeeze.

"That would indicate you're tone deaf—which goes a long way towards explaining that performance, which was ghastly. Simply ghastly. You have no more chance of winning this contest than I have of becoming Miss Universe."

The crowd booed.

"I guess that means Rodney wants to wear a tiara," quipped Breeze.

The amplified voice of the director broke in over the PA system. "Uh, Brian, that putdown doesn't really work. Could you try another?"

"Oh...okay," Breeze said, releasing Ricky. His brow

furrowed in thought, he looked at the stage. "Any ideas?" he finally asked. Looking toward the control booth.

Suggestions, many of them quite nasty, were shouted out by the audience.

"Oh, for Christ's sake," snarled Rodney. "Just say, 'Well, we know Rodney won't be winning Miss Congeniality.'"

Breeze looked questioningly up toward the booth. "Works for me," announced the director. And in two takes, we had our ad lib.

On and on we went with this comedy of horrors, each singer worse than the last. The only finalists who were halfway bearable were Cletus, who powered through "Working for a Livin'" like a blacksmith coaxing a bellows, and, I hate to admit it, Bobby. Getting one of the better songs in the Lewis canon, "The Heart of Rock & Roll," no doubt helped, but Bobby also had an ease on camera that, at this stage in the competition, none of the other contestants did.

Far and away the best pure vocal performance was by Shontika, who brought a surprising gospel feel to "The Power of Love." There was power and pride in her voice that reminded me of Patti LaBelle.

All ten singers gathered onstage for the final shot. Before the cameras were turned on, Brian quickly reshuffled their order so the smallest were flanking him. Just as the director shouted, "Action," a woman who looked like a heavier version of Eva ran up the center aisle past the judges' table, clutching a little girl by the arm. She practically threw the kid up on the stage. Eva leaned over and patted her knees like she was encouraging a dog and the girl ran to her, hugging her leg. Eva stroked the kid's hair, beaming at the camera.

Brian announced, "There you have it. The ten finalists. Who stays and who goes—it's up to you. You have to vote for your favorite. The phone lines are now open. We'll be back with the results tomorrow."

The brash *Star Maker* music began to play. It sounded like the theme from an all-news radio station. Brian barked, "Call me the Breeze," and everyone onstage waved and smiled to beat the band.

The tableau reminded me of the way every episode of *The Dating Game* ended. But I'd trade ten Brian Breezes for one Jim Lange.

As the song faded, Roxie turned to me, eyes twinkling, and said, "I smell Emmy."

"I smell something," I replied.

Family and friends of the contestants made their way up to the stage. Cletus dwarfed his parents, wiry farm types who looked distinctly uncomfortable in the spotlights. Patsy was in the grip of a guy who looked like a seedier version of Pat Sajak. He was hugging her so tight I thought he would crush her. There was a look of elation on his flushed face. If you can be drunk with pride, he was.

Eva peeled the child off her leg and handed her back to her inflated clone. She threw herself on a skinny guy with badly dyed coal-black hair who made Britney Spears's husband Kevin Federline look rugged.

"What was that all about?" I asked Roxie.

"You mean the little girl?"

I nodded.

"All the baby mommas on the show do that—pull their kid up onstage. They think it gets them the sympathy vote."

"Does it work?"

"Yeah, but it's a trump card you can usually play only once, though. There's a backlash if you keep doing it. The audience feels manipulated. Eva played it right off the bat. She must really be desperate."

"Matt's roommate John told me no boyfriends allowed."

"Yeah, she'll get reprimanded for that. But he wasn't seen on camera anyway."

"So what happens now?"

"Well, the contestants take turns in the press room before they get shuttled back to the house. And there's a production meeting upstairs where Rodney, Ian and the director recap the show."

"I'd like to hear that session."

"Let's go," she said, indicating the direction as if she were heading a soccer ball.

Only a few stragglers were left onstage as we crossed through to the rehearsal room. Rows of folding chairs had been set up in front of a podium. Behind it hung a curtain emblazoned with the *Star Maker* logo. A handful of reporters were scattered among enough seats to accommodate the White House press corps. I recognized the guy from *USA Today* in the first row.

Flushed and happy, Patsy was taking her turn in front of the mic. Standing next to her and still beaming was the strip-mall Sajak. "I think we all respect Rodney," she was saying. "He's just trying to prod us to do our best. It's a form of tough love."

"Were you nervous tonight?" called out an Asian woman.

"Very nervous. I think we all were. It's like opening-night jitters. But I'm just so glad my dad was here to share it with me," she said, turning to her companion.

"Could he answer a question?" a bored-sounding voice boomed, like a customer in a diner berating the waiter because there was no ketchup at his booth.

Patsy extended a hand and her father charged up to join

her, so eager he hit his mouth against the microphone, setting off a wail of feedback.

"So what'd you think, Mr. Harris?"

"Oh, gee. I was just so proud. You know I haven't always been there for Patsy. I missed so much. So I'm so glad to see her get this chance. She's just so darned talented."

Roxie and I walked to the adjoining hallway. "What was that all about?" I asked as we climbed the cinderblock stairwell.

"I feel so sorry for Patsy," she said. "That was her father, Lenny. The guy was a real bad junkie and was in jail almost the whole time she was growing up. She didn't even know him, really."

We reached the second floor and headed down the corridor past the James Arness Employee Lounge. "Then Patsy gets this break and guess who turns up, just out of a jail and supposedly reformed. She's such a sweetheart. Of course she welcomes him right back into her life."

Roxie shook her head ruefully. I didn't say anything because it was obvious where her allegiance lay. Me, I firmly believed in giving the junkie a second chance. But then, I belong to the villains, thieves and scoundrels union.

Without knocking, Roxie opened the door to the Edward R. Murrow Conference Room. Compared to the other spaces I had seen in this building, this was a broom closet. So much for the stature of newsmen.

Ian and Rodney sat at opposite ends of a coffin-shaped table, their assistants hovering behind them. Sandy Bauer, the show's musical coordinator, the woman who coached the singers on their performances, sat to Ian's right. She looked upset. I would too if I had a hand in that musical atrocity.

To Ian's left sat a heavy-set owl-faced man with a graying beard and hair. Roxie later identified him as Stan Jacobs, the *Star Maker* director.

I had already discerned his role. He was, after all, sporting the TV directors' colors: a baseball cap pulled down tightly on his head and a profoundly unhappy expression on his face.

An apoplectic Rodney held the floor. "We can't go through a season like this. This is unquestionably the weakest batch we've ever had!"

"You say that every season, Rodney," pointed out Sandy.

"And every year it gets worse. Were you listening tonight, Sandy? That was bloody awful. Who do think is going to watch those tossers?"

"About twenty-five million Americans?" ventured Stan.

"Oh, button it, Stan. It's easy for you. You have no interest in the back end. I have to take one of these bloody toads and sell them as a legitimate recording artist. Who do you think is going to buy the Ricky Tavares bloody Christmas collection?"

"God help us," muttered Ian. I was glad to see the pressure of producing the season's first big show hadn't interfered with his drinking schedule. He was blotto.

"They'll be fine, Rodney," said Sandy. "The worst ones will be eliminated like they always are and we'll be left with a strong nucleus."

"Are you out of your fucking mind? There are no good singers in that lot. Not one."

"You wouldn't be talking this way if Matt had been on that stage," said Stan.

"Well, Matt's not fucking here, is he? Leaving us with bloody fuck-all. Not only that, we have the worst singers on the planet chirping away on the worst songs ever written. Huey Bloody Lewis! Sandy, you've got to be kidding me."

Sandy sighed. "Rodney, we've been over this. Everything we could get the rights to we drove into the ground in the first three seasons. The audience burned out on Whitney Houston, Luther Vandross and Motown. The only quality material left is prohibitively expensive."

"Great. So what's next week? Neil fucking Diamond?"

She hesitated. "Actually, it's Glen Campbell," she said quietly.

"Great bloody hell! You're trying to fucking kill me, aren't you?" Rodney bellowed. "Do you have any idea who watches this ponsey show? Teenage girls, that's who. They think Gwen Stefani is decrepit. I'm forty-three years old and I can't think of a single Glen Campbell song. Do you think our audience will have the foggiest idea who they're listening to?"

"'Witchita Lineman,'" ventured Stan.

"What?" Rodney asked, as if he couldn't believe his ears.

"It's a Glen Campbell song."

"Right. Listen, Stan, if I want to hear from you again during this meeting, I will squeeze your fat, livery lips. Now SHUT UP!"

"Honestly, Rodney, Campbell was very big in the States," said Sandy.

"In what bloody century? Look, Sandy, your job is to secure us music that our audience will have some familiarity with, however vague. And you're going backwards. We're about two weeks away from doing Gregorian bloody chants."

He took a deep, huffy breath. "I'm putting you on notice, Sandy. Ian, I want you to mark this. If you don't get us some contemporary material—and soon—you're going to be back doing trade shows in Tarzana!"

He pushed back from the table, scowling.

"Where are you going, Rodney?" asked Ian, his rheumy eyes rolling in their wattled sockets.

"To play golf," he said, and headed for the door, assistant on his heels.

"It's ten o'clock at night, old boy."

"Then I'll knock around some balls at the driving range. I've got to get out of here."

As he exited, I turned to Roxie. "We can go too."

Out in the corridor, I told her, "Much as I was enjoying that session, I don't think it's going to help me find who killed Matt."

"Oh, I wouldn't rule out Glen Campbell as a suspect," she said, making me smile.

Back down in the press room, Neveah had just replaced Flip at the podium.

"So you've changed your name, Robin?" asked a semi-recumbent reporter in the back row.

"That's right," she said brightly. "I am now officially and legally Neveah."

"So is it Neveah Cracknell?" asked Dan Rubowski.

"No, just Neveah. One name. Like Madonna. Or Ricky."

"Ricky who?" asked the Asian woman.

"Ricky Martin."

That response hung in the room for a few seconds.

"Just for the record, could you spell Neveah?" asked Rubowski, pencil poised above notebook.

"Sure. It's N...E...V...E...A...H. That's heaven spelled backwards," she said, with a victorious smile.

"Umm, actually it's not. Heaven backwards would be Nevaeh."

"Shit," said Neveah disgustedly. "Are you sure?"

All the reporters' heads started bobbing quickly.

"All right, then spell it... that other way."

A network publicist hustled over to Neveah's side. They held a hurried and whispered conference which everyone in the room could hear over the microphone.

"You can't change it again, Neveah. It's already recorded with the state as your professional name. It's also on our website and it went out in a national release. And that's the way it's spelled on your contract."

"But it's spelled wrong," she whined.

"Too late."

"Damn it." She turned back to the reporters, who were leaning forward, hanging on her next words. "All right, it's N...E...V...E...A...H. That's almost like heaven spelled backwards."

Back in the auditorium, there was no sign of Whitey. I had Roxie drop me back at my hotel. Up in my room, I set about washing the bad *Star Maker* music out of my ears. I put Earth Wind & Fire's "Be Ever Wonderful" on Repeat and listened to it happily over and over again until it was Maurice White's voice echoing in my head—not Ricky Tavares's.

I woke up the next morning with a headache, a hard-on and a charlie horse. All I need, I mused as I limped toward the bathroom, is a hunchback and I could make some mad scientist a lovely lab assistant.

But starting off the day badly doesn't bother me. Fate, in my experience, tends to be even-handed. Things usually balance out by dinnertime.

I didn't have to wait that long. Detective Mike Klingelhof called while I was having breakfast at the Farmers Market, leaving me a message that he would talk to me at his office at robbery-homicide at noon.

A few hours later, a bare-headed Whitey picked me up in his lender Escalade to drive me to the Parker Center. "What happened to the beret, lucky Pierre?"

He shrugged. "It was an experiment. I thought chicks would dig it. Turns out it only appealed to the ones with borderline personalities."

"So where'd you disappear to after the taping last night? We looked all over for you."

"I was following up a lead."

I looked over at him skeptically, waiting for the punch line. There was none. He kept his eyes focused on the road.

I leaned back into the leather captain's chair. These Escalades may look garish, but I have to admit, they make a nice ride.

"Whitey, do I need to remind you you're working for me? What kind of lead are we talking?"

From the side, I could see his right eye squint behind his round blue sunglasses. "Did you see that sleazeball guy who was hugging that punk girl, Eva?"

"Yeah?"

"I got a bad vibe off him. So I followed him."

"And what did you find out?"

"He took Eva to a hip-hop club in North Hollywood. He drives a beat-up old Camaro that's had more bodywork than Pam Anderson. Then he took her back to a dump he shares with three other losers south of the airport. I'd be willing to bet they're all meth addicts."

"Why?"

"The way they look. The hours they keep. The visitors they get."

"And what do we make of this, Super Snoop?"

"Just another card to add to the deck. But it's interesting, don't you think? Speed freaks are a depraved species, man. It's like living in a zombie movie."

"You find out his name?"

"Jimmy Ayoub. Got it off the registration in his glove box while he was in the club. His friends call him Jammy."

"All right," I said. "We'll have to keep an eye on Jammy. So what'd you think of the taping?"

"I think," he said, hitting his signal for the Alameda Avenue exit, "that *Star Maker* needs a new announcer. And I think Shontika was by far the best singer."

"Same."

"Apparently we're not alone. The odds on Shontika went from twenty-five-to-one to three-to-one overnight."

"How? The show hasn't aired yet."

"I guess there were a couple of spies in the crowd."

"You wouldn't happen to be one of those spies, would you, Whitey? Maybe you helped set the line." For a guy who didn't gamble himself, Whitey had had extensive betting contacts for as long as I knew him.

He pursed his lips and shook his head. "Nah. I'm no judge of singing talent. No one's going to take a flyer on my say-so. But it is valuable information. Especially this early in the competition when none of these kids have much of a track record. Anyway," he said, looking over his shoulder as he pulled over to the curb across from the LAPD building, "Shontika Mason is your new *Star Maker* favorite. You want me to come in with you?"

"No," I said. "I don't want to do anything to get the detective cranky. But this could take a while. Why don't you hit a meeting and I'll call you when I'm ready to go?" I climbed out and spoke to him through the open passenger window. "I want to drive out to the contestants' house before the show airs tonight."

"If you're meeting the finalists, get Roxie to drive you," he said. "I don't want to be seen with you." I watched his car pull out into traffic. I'm sure he didn't mean that the way it sounded.

I was early for my appointment, which was fortunate because two hours later I was still sitting on a bench outside Klingelhof's squad office.

Finally, a heavyset guy with close-cropped hair and

wary eyes stepped into the corridor and jerked his thumb at me. I imagined that was the gesture that Roxie's father, the school principal, used to summon truants into his office. Klingelhof was stocky and virtually neckless, with a rounded back that rose up to thick, ursine shoulders. But I noticed as I walked behind him that his step was springy and his suit pants and his expensive dress shirt were tailored to fit his unconventional shape.

He led me to his metal desk in a bullpen area with nearly a dozen other desks. Only one other detective was at his station, peering into a computer screen and then looking down at his fingers to type. The phones were ringing constantly on all the desks, but I guess voice mail and cell phones had done away with the need for a receptionist.

There was a captain's office at the far end of the room, against the outer wall, but the door was closed and filing cabinets blocked all but the top of the glass partition, so I couldn't see if anyone was inside.

"Sorry for the delay. I had some breaking developments on a case," he said, smirking to indicate that it was bullshit, that he had let me wait just to bust my balls. I wondered if Klingelhof and Whitey were buying their dialogue from the same hack.

He sat at his desk, hunched over, his fingers crossed. "So what can I do for you, *Mr.* McNamara?"

"As I think you know, I'm looking into Matt Hanes's death. I was hoping you might share with me whatever your investigation turned up—any evidence, any suspects."

He nodded and smiled with mock agreeability. "I got nothing," he said, opening his palms. "Your friends at the network froze our investigation before it got started. They preferred someone with your expertise. Someone who wouldn't inconvenience their busy schedule."

Inwardly I sighed. This was not going to be easy. "But you visited the crime scene?" I asked.

"Yeah. We generally try to rouse ourselves when there's a homicide."

"I'm sure there's an autopsy report and results from your crime techs. May I see those?"

He tilted his head, a gesture that said, *Get serious.*

I played the only trump card I had—the name I had gotten from Mitch Reynolds. "Look, Detective, I fully agree that the smarter course would have been to let you pursue your investigation, but I'm just trying to do my job. And I was assured by Chief Cavanaugh that I would have your full cooperation."

I could see the clouds boil up in Klingelhof's eyes as he calculated the import of this threat. Cops get fairly macho when their turf is being trampled by a rank outsider like me, but they're also bureaucrats. In truth I had never spoken with Cavanaugh. I was just throwing his name into the conversation like a concussion grenade.

"Could you just walk me quickly through what you did find out?"

It took a few seconds for Klingelhof to stow away the defiance he had greeted me with. When he answered, there was a new businesslike neutrality to his tone.

"I don't know much and it's all fairly straightforward," he said, bristling his hair with one hand. "And just so you know, I'm not giving you any files that are proprietary to this department unless you have a release signed by my captain." He jerked his thumb at the office behind him.

I nodded. He nodded. "Okay, no witnesses. No one saw anyone entering or leaving his room. Detectives canvassed all the guests on that floor and everyone in the lobby. Nothing. Time of death approximately twenty-two thirty. Caused by asphyxiation. The hotel pillow. No other marks or bruises. It's unlikely he put up much of a struggle. He was probably incapacitated, judging by the amount of flunitrazepam we found in his system.

"There was a pizza in the room which tested for flunitrazepam. The decedent ate three slices. That's how much was gone from the pie and that's how much the coroner found in his stomach. So he didn't have company for dinner. No signs of forced entry."

"Security camera footage?"

He shook his head. "Only on the loading dock in back. Nothing there."

"Any fingerprint evidence?"

"The decedent's prints were all over the place—on the door handle, the table, the bedboard, the bathroom, you name it. Of course, you eat pizza every night like this guy apparently did, you become a fingerprint machine because of all the grease that collects in your whorls."

"How about on the pillow?"

He laughed. It wasn't infectious. "Little piece of advice, McNamara? Next time you check into a hotel, bring your own linens. They don't do a very sanitary job down in your average hotel laundry. We found more than fifty partials on that one pillowcase alone. Ran all the viable ones though NCB. No hits."

Uh, yuck.

"The pizza was delivered, right?" I asked.

"Yeah, the doorman and a front desk clerk both remember the pizza guy pulling up in front sometime after nine and walking with his delivery sack back to the elevator. Same as most nights. The decedent was apparently a regular customer. Delivery guy left a few minutes later."

"Did you talk to him?"

"Nope."

"Why not?"

"Me and my partner were waiting for his next shift to start when we got the order to stand down."

"Can I have the delivery guy's name and where he works?"

Klingelhof opened a very thin dark brown folder on his desk and perused a document. "The delivery guy's name is Don Walmsley. Works at Slice of Heaven on La Cienaga."

"All right, Detective. I appreciate your cooperation. Before I go, is there anything else you wanted to say?"

He frowned. "Only that it's annoying as hell to have this snatched away from us. The killer would be sitting in a jail cell right now if they let us do our job."

"And who do you think that killer is?"

"Whoever sprinkled the Rohypnol on his goddamn pizza."

I nodded. "Anything else?"

He looked at me, weighing something in his mind. "I hesitated to mention this. I'm still not sure what it means. But it looked like—and the coroner agrees—that the kid died with a smile on his face. Never seen that before."

I made my way downstairs to call Roxie. The problem with not having a cell is that you have to depend on pay phones, and they're increasingly hard to find.

Twenty minutes after I reached her, Roxie pulled up in front of the Parker Center. "Where to, Cappy?" She was wearing a tight blue, short-sleeve button-up blouse that pinched her torso, and a short khaki skirt. Her hair looked like she was fresh from the shower.

"Take me out to the *Star Makers* house," I said, belting in. "But could we make a stop at Linens-n-Things first?"

Could I ask you a question?" asked Roxie as we climbed into the hills.

"Sure," I said encouragingly. I was feeling magnanimous, with my bags of lovely new bedding and towels rustling in the back seat.

"Would it be all right if I went to an AA meeting with you, or is that not allowed?"

"No, it's fine, as long as it's an open meeting. Anyone can go to those. There are closed meetings that you have to be an alcoholic to attend."

"Is that where you do the pagan rituals?" she jibed.

"No, it's not like that. But AA can be pretty confessional. So there have to be meetings where we can feel safe, meetings where we can unload our darkest secrets."

"Sounds torturous," she said, wincing. She looked really cute when she wrinkled her nose.

"It's therapeutic, really," I responded. "We have a saying in the program: You're only as sick as your secrets."

She drove for a while without speaking.

"May I ask why you want to go to a meeting?" I asked.

"I've never known anyone in AA, at least as far as I know. And," she said with a tight grin, "I wanted to see what makes a guy like you tick."

I addressed the safe part of that statement.

"That surprises me," I said. "I thought everybody had at least one drunk falling out of their family tree. My family is rotten with them."

"Not mine," she said. "When we have our family reunion every summer, the only thing they serve is lemonade. I mean, there's a few AA meetings in my town, and a ton of them in Davenport. But I just didn't know anyone who went. And I guess I've always had preconceptions of what it's like. So I thought you could help me check it out."

"Well, you're welcome at open meetings. You can go with me or Whitey or even by yourself."

I saw a little frown tug at her mouth. I wasn't sure what I had said wrong and I didn't have time to ask. We were being waved up the drive by a different set of guards, two guys who looked like Aztec executioners behind their sunglasses.

"Listen, Roxie, I want to make sure all ten of these singers are alibied for the night of Matt's murder. Could you ask whoever handled Greg's travel arrangements how sure we can be of his whereabouts? I need that really nailed down."

"I'll take care of it," she said briskly. Definite cold front coming off Ms. Bena.

The house was a hive of activity. It was less than two hours until the first finals show aired. I had imagined they would all watch it together, but almost everyone was getting ready to go out. Makes sense, I guess. You don't want to be sitting home when your fifteen minutes of fame arrive.

I began picking off the singers randomly as they crossed my path, asking them about their memories of going out to the restaurant together the night Matt died. Who could they remember being there? What made them sure? Who had sat to their right, to their left? I used the pad I carry to sketch out a little seating plan.

There were three people I had particular issues with. Flip was the first one I flagged down. As always, he was orbiting Cletus. I took Flip into the deserted dining room. After taking him through the same questions I was asking everyone, I said, "So I understand you and Matt got into it."

"Who told you that?" he asked, his hackles up immediately.

I shrugged. "What was it about?"

"This is bullshit," he shouted. "You got a houseful of muthafuckas got just as much reason to kill Matt as me, but who you settle on? Sweat the black man, right? I shoulda known. Whole houseful of people, but the nigga musta done it. That how you work, CrackNamara?"

I kept cool through his rant. "What was the fight about, Flip?"

"Like you don't fucking know. Whoever told you we fought, told you it was over some piece of shit jewelry he says I took from his room. The door's always open in him and John's room. People going in and out all night long, but he figures I must be the one took it."

"I'm beginning to see a pattern here, Flip."

"You see whatever you want, slick. But you ain't fooling me. You ask Clete. I told him as soon as you showed up that you was gonna try to pin this on me or Greg."

I didn't pay much attention to Flip's accusations. I don't like to think of myself as a racist. But when I was mulling it over later, I had to admit that Greg and Flip were near the top of my list of suspects. What put them there—logic or social conditioning—I really wasn't sure.

My encounters with the other two were even briefer.

"I understand you had a few run-ins with Matt," I said to Eva.

She smirked. "What a choirboy. He wanted everything to be fair and square. Why wouldn't he? The deck was like completely stacked in his favor. I kept telling him it was a competition. And if he got in my way, there were going to be sneaker prints going up his ass. This is my big chance and I'm going for it."

I nodded. "You going to watch the show with your daughter?"

She shook her head. "She's with my sister. I'm going to a viewing party some radio station is holding."

"Is Jammy going with you?"

Her look became guarded. "How do you know my boyfriend's name?"

I shrugged. "That's part of my job. Finding out who all the players are. How long have you known him?"

"About a month. As if it's any of your business. Met him at a club just a few nights after *Star Maker* flew me out here."

"So is he picking you up tonight?"

"No. I got lectured today by one of the associate producers. Any *Star Maker*–related events I have to keep up the illusion that I'm single. Jammy can go to the shows if he wants, but he can't come up on the stage afterwards." She tilted her head and looked at me sideways. "But you already knew I was called on the rug, didn't you?" Before I could object, she said, "Whatever. I'm out of here." She started to scurry from the room, then turned. "By the way, I wouldn't push your luck with Jammy and his friends. They don't take kindly to people getting up in their business."

Probably a good policy for men with their proclivities.

I caught my final mark as he was slipping out the door. "Yo, Bobby," I called, stepping outside after him. He looked at me as you would a persistent panhandler.

"You find that girl who was with you the night Matt died?"

"Not yet." He pulled a comb out of his shirt pocket and began to lightly feather his hair, never taking his eyes from mine.

"You better get on that, bra. Seriously."

"Yeah, yeah."

"Listen, I understand you had words with Matt."

"You talked to John, huh?"

"Why do you say that?"

"Because we only *had words*," he said, crooking his fingers to indicate quotation marks, "on two occasions. And John was in the room both times."

"What was it about?"

"Stupid shit. Both times he was warning me to leave Patsy alone. Which was ridiculous, but Matt liked playing the white knight. All I ever did was flirt with the girl. I wasn't trying to nail her. I like almost all kinds of women, but not the shy, virginal types. It's not worth the effort. Let someone else break 'em in."

As we spoke, an economy rental car pulled into the big turnaround below us. Patsy and her father got out. He embraced her, got back in, and as he headed back down the driveway, shouted out, "Good luck tonight, Pats."

Bobby began walking down the stairs toward Patsy. "I'll tell you who I would like to see naked underneath me, though," he said, looking back at me and smiling lasciviously. "Your friend Roxie. That girl is not as innocent as she looks. Know what I mean... bra?"

He headed toward a canary-yellow Volkswagen convertible with two girls chattering excitedly in the front seat. Bobby said something to Patsy as he passed her, but she didn't seem to hear him, practically skipping up the stairs.

"Hi, Mr. McNamara," she said, beaming. "Great day, huh?"

I squinted up at the haze sitting atop the city like the foam on a cappuccino. Seemed like any other day in the L.A. kiln to me.

"How are you, Patsy?"

"Really, really good," she said, leaning on the railing next to me and taking a deep, luxuriant breath. Below us, the Volkswagen fizzed away, trailing laughter.

"This show has been such a gift to me. I honestly don't care if I win or not. It's given me my father back. And that's incredibly precious to me. I just spent the afternoon with him. I haven't been able to do that since I was eight years old. We went to the Santa Monica pier."

"I'm happy for you."

"Thanks. Hey, someone told me you were in AA," she said, then looked abashed. "Oh, gee, am I not supposed to say that? Am I spoiling your anonymity?"

"No, it's fine, Patsy. I'm pretty public about being in recovery."

"Good, because I think it's so admirable. It's nothing short of miraculous what it's done for my father. He was lost to us. And now he's back. Well, my mother still isn't talking to him, but she'll come around. I know I prayed for him every day that he was in jail and it's like my prayers have been answered."

"I'm happy for both of you."

"How long have you been in AA, Mr. McNamara?"

"Nearly eight years."

"Wow, that's incredible. Your family must be so proud of you."

I nodded and managed a compliant smile. The truth was this conversation was making me uncomfortable. Sure, I was grateful to be sober. But I didn't consider it a mark of distinction or a sign of strong character. Alcohol and drugs had thoroughly kicked my ass and taken every last shred of dignity I possessed.

AA was a desperate last resort when all else had failed and all hope was gone. Not that I was unusual in that regard. An old-timer at my first home group at the Perry Street clubhouse in downtown Manhattan used to say, "No one comes into these rooms whistling 'Camptown Ladies.'"

I certainly understood Patsy's enthusiasm, but it was jarring for me. Sort of like being commended for being on the losing side of a battle. And it followed so closely on Roxie's curiosity about AA. It always felt a little awkward discussing the program with earthlings.

Oh, and just for the record, following a mean distillation process, my family essentially boils down to my mother. About once a year, she'll inquire in disparaging tones if I'm "still going to those meetings."

If she's proud of my sobriety, she's keeping it pretty well disguised.

"There oughta be rules," I said sourly as Whitey and I walked back to his car after a seven A.M. meeting in West Hollywood the next morning. Knowing our evening would probably be absorbed by the live *Star Maker* show, at the end of which one contestant would be eliminated, we had arranged to go early.

"Dude," he said. "It's AA. There are rules."

"Well, there should be more rules."

"Such as?" he said, humoring me.

"No talking about pets. I'm sure that lady's Pomeranian is perfectly lovable and I'm sorry to learn about all the health problems the little fella has had, but I don't want to hear her sob about them for five minutes. What do I look like, a veterinary grief counselor? Your dog is sick, lady. Get over it."

"People really care about their pets."

"Fine. Let them form some other goddamn program

and share about it there. What does it have to do with me staying sober today?"

"Somebody hasn't had their morning coffee yet."

"Uggh, the coffee in there was undrinkable. Did you taste it? That should be another rule: If you can't master something as simple as making coffee, don't volunteer for that service. Let someone else do it. Because I don't want to swallow Drāno first thing in the morning. That reminds me, you know who I saw back by the kitchen when I was dumping out that poison they call coffee? Patsy's father."

"Patsy the *Star Maker* contestant?" Whitey asked. We had reached his car and were talking across the roof.

"Yeah."

Just as a point of order, I would never normally reveal the identity of anyone I saw at a meeting. You didn't hear me bring up the names of the two sitcom stars from different networks who were also at that meeting, even though one of them shared a funny anecdote about what an alkie George C. Scott had been. But I can't tell the story of this case without revealing that I saw Patsy's father that morning.

I filled Whitey in on my visit to the house and my survey results as we drove to breakfast. "Except for Bobby and Greg, they were all together at that restaurant the night Matt was killed. Unless they're conspiring together to provide an alibi for one or more of them. But that seems unlikely to me."

"So we're looking at Bobby and Greg?"

"Not necessarily. It just means the other eight can account for their whereabouts. That doesn't mean they weren't involved in Matt's death. The more I see of Eva, for instance, the more convinced I am she wouldn't hesitate to have someone killed to win that recording contract. I just wonder if she has the money to afford a hit man."

"There's other ways to pay a guy than cash," Whitey

pointed out. "And I guarantee you, for Jammy and his friends, life is cheap."

"You should have seen Patsy, though. She was so proud of her old man."

"I hope the fucker has it together to stay sober. I'd hate to see her hopes get crushed."

"Well, I'm glad we saw him at a meeting," I said. "That's a sign he's serious. Speaking of meetings, you know who wants to check out a meeting? Roxie. You should take her to an open meeting this week."

Whitey had pulled into the small cindered parking lot of the place he said had "the best waffles on the West Coast." The building looked like a porch that had been torn off a hotel. It was about the dimensions of one of those Slipstream trailer luncheonettes, but it was wood with a pitched, tiled roof.

He put the car in park and looked at me with disbelief. "How dense are you, Mac?" I awaited amplification. "She doesn't want to go to a meeting with me, you idiot." He pulled his hand slowly down his face, stretching the skin. "Roxie asked me how she could get to know you better. I suggested the accelerated course would be going to a meeting with you, because recovery is a lot of who you are. I can't believe I have to explain this to you. Roxie isn't—"

Whitey's cell phone went off. Unless I was mistaken, the ringtone was "Perdido." He looked at the display. "Speak of the angel and up she pops." He flipped up the faceplate. "Hey, Roxie, we were just...Okay, I understand. we'll be right over."

He threw the phone on the seat, put his sunglasses back on and turned the key in the ignition with force, as if he expected resistance. "Roxie said all hell has broken loose. They need us over at Tootsi Frootsi right away." He threw the car into reverse and swept, bouncing, out into the street.

For a moment, I felt like I was in an episode of *Starsky and Hutch*. Personally, I would have opted for the waffles. Good news is worth dropping everything for and rushing over. You never know how long that will last. But bad news? Not worth hustling to meet. It's always waiting patiently when you get there.

Whitey knew every shortcut in the city and he used most of them—including cutting across gas-station lots—as he raced over to Universal City. But even he couldn't entirely circumvent Los Angeles' morning rush hour.

We definitely should have had the waffles, I thought, as we whizzed past the loading docks behind a strip mall.

The offices of Tootsi Frootsi were in a gleaming glass and steel complex across from City Walk atop the promontory in Universal City. A worried-looking Roxie, her hair pulled back in a French braid, met us in the lobby and ushered us upstairs, briefly filling us in on the stairwell.

"It was a bad day to start with," she said. "We had the lowest vote count ever last night. Then the overnights came in and the ratings numbers were down too. Mitch came in breathing fire and called a honchos-only meeting. No one knows what it's about, but Ian's assistant came out almost immediately and told me they wanted you over here right away."

As we approached the glassed-in conference room, I could see Mitch, Ian and Rodney along with two other young-executive types I didn't recognize sitting at an oblong table. The usual ring of subalterns surrounded them. Judging by their intense, strained expressions, voices were being raised, but the room must have been soundproofed, because we could hear nothing.

Roxie opened the door for us and followed us into the room. "Who's this?" growled Ian, pointing his chin at Whitey. I wish I had a picture of Ian that morning. I'd take it out and study it when the urges to drink or snort some coke emerged from the basement where I keep them chained up. In the morning light Braithwait was a poster boy for the ravages of alcohol. He looked like an unfinished jigsaw puzzle that had been abandoned and left out in the rain.

"This is my associate Whitey...Stahl." Funny thing about 12-step programs. You get used to dealing with people exclusively by their first names. Often that's all you know. It took me a minute to retrieve Whitey's full name. "You can speak freely in front of him. What's up, gentlemen?"

"We lost Shontika," said Mitch.

"What do you mean, *lost*?"

"She's off the show," Ian said.

"Why? What happened?"

"We got a fax at seven this morning with a detailed history of her arrest record—and it's extensive," said Mitch. He was so angry, the skin below his left eye was twitching. "The fax went on to say that if Shontika is still in the competition after tonight's results show, the information will be sent to the Smoking Gun website."

"May I see the fax?" I asked.

Scowling, Mitch slid a green file folder the length of the table. One of the two network suits handed it back to me. I pulled the fax out and perused it, with Whitey practically breathing on my neck as he read over my shoulder. There was a list of arrests for a Mary Mason with the dates and charges. It looked like she was part of a smash-and-grab crew hitting jewelry stores in the Chicago area—a not very successful crew, judging by how often they got collared. There were also a smattering of assault and battery, resisting arrest and trafficking in stolen goods charges.

"Have you confirmed this is true? Is Shontika Mary?"

"Jerry?" said Mitch, pointing his chin at the other exec at the table. The guy looked like Rob Lowe wearing severe European-style rimless glasses.

"I went to the house and woke up Shontika as soon as Mitch notified me," said Jerry. "She professed her innocence for a while, but eventually she admitted that she was in fact Mary. That's only her adult record, by the way. Apparently she was active as a juvenile as well. My office is working on retrieving that information."

"Why do we have to go through this every bloody year?" asked Rodney. "I thought we had tightened up the screening process."

"We did," protested Jerry. His corporate buddy nodded emphatically. "But she changed her name and her birth date on the application. She presented a driver's license with consistent data. Obviously that was falsified."

"We'd do better just recruiting singers directly out of Leavenworth," said Mitch. His voice went up almost an octave when he was angry. "I want you to go back over the other contestants again. Thorough background checks. I do not want a repeat of season three."

I leaned over and whispered to Roxie, "What happened in season three?" Her hair smelled of chamomile shampoo.

"Three of the finalists had felony convictions."

I whistled silently.

"I think Ian's recommendation is clearly our best course to minimize the damage," said Mitch. "Unless someone has a better idea?"

"What is Ian's plan?" I asked aloud.

"Shontika will be eliminated tonight as the lowest vote-getter," said Rodney.

"Was she? The lowest?"

"No, it was Greg and—what's that ridiculous trollop's name?—Neveah. They finished in a virtual dead heat," said Ian. "It was to have been Neveah's neck on the chopping block tonight."

"Can you do that? Misrepresent the voting totals?" My questions drew a round of chuckles at the table. I blushed at my naïveté. "Don't you have an accounting firm that certifies the votes?"

"Jim, have you met Richard?" Ian asked. The exec who had handed me the fax half turned and saluted. "Jerry and Richard are our lawyers. But Richard has another job as well. Once a season we push him out onstage under a pseudonym and introduce him to America as the head of an independent accounting firm."

"The numbers are what we say they are," Mitch said. "And tonight Shontika loses. If we take this legit, we would lose Neveah on votes and Shontika on scandal. Two eliminations, leaving us with eight finalists and nine weeks of shows. And we can't afford to fill a week with crappy clip specials. The ratings were bad enough last night as it is. Which reminds me: Everyone stay in their seats after this meeting is over, everyone but Jim and his people, Jerry and Richard. We have to have a serious discussion about the numbers."

"Do it my way and we rid ourselves of Shontika without taking a black eye over her sordid past," Ian said. "America has spoken." He was surprisingly lucid in the morning.

When Whitey spoke, it startled me because he had been silent during the entire meeting.

"Excuse me, but why?" he asked. Most of the heads in the room turned to look at him. Ian, I noticed, seemed to be studying his navel. Lucid but not too limber.

"Why did someone send this fax?" Whitey continued. "You want Shontika off the show and you have her criminal record. Why not give it to the *L.A. Times* or Smoking Gun? That accomplishes what you're after. Why give the show a chance to save face? Why not just drop the hammer?"

An obvious answer occurred to me, although I didn't share it aloud. If you were a *Star Maker* contestant trying to manipulate the process in your favor, an anonymous, threatening fax might be the way to go. That way you get the producers to do your dirty work and eliminate the frontrunner without a trail leading back to you.

Meanwhile, the room was still pondering Whitey's question. Then Mitch said, "Perhaps we'll get the answer to that when Mr. McNamara finds out who sent it. Now, if you'll excuse us, we need to get down to the nasty business of television. Take the fax with you, please."

As we left the room, I saw an envelope propped on a plastic stand. Written in handsome calligraphy, it read: "2006 Winner...Mr. Braithwait's Prediction."

Boy, if he actually gets this one right, I thought, he should have his own show, because he's clearly better than the psychic charlatans currently on the tube.

CHAPTER 19

Whitey went off to trace the fax. He had a friend at the phone company who was going to find the location of the number it was sent from. Roxie drove me back to the hotel.

"You know," she said, as we walked through the *Petticoat Junction* décor of the lobby, "your hotel is the only one in Los Angeles that I always feel overdressed in."

"I don't know. It's starting to grow on me. I'm thinking of taking up square dancing."

"I could give you lessons," she said.

I glanced over to see if she was pulling my leg. She was looking straight-faced at the floor numbers above the door in the elevator as they lit up.

"I meant to tell you, it looks like Greg checks out," she said when we were in my room. "The woman who handles the travel arrangements for the contestants went over his itinerary. He flew home the morning that Matt died. One of our designated chaperones went to LAX with him. We called him in Florida the following day to ask him to return. He was on a flight from West Palm that night."

"Okay, thanks," I said. I have to admit I was a little disappointed. Not that I had a hard-on for Greg, but I always harbor a hope that these cases will solve themselves.

There was a message light blinking on my phone. "Jim, it's your mother. Thanks for remembering my birthday."

"Shit," I exclaimed. Lost track of the date again. I just assumed my mother was being sarcastic because it would be entirely in keeping with the castigative way she usually communicated with me. But as the message continued, I realized she was being sincere. It sounded so odd coming out of her mouth.

"It's such a beautiful mantilla. Is that what they call it? Anyway it's a lovely gift. And so thoughtful. And actually on time for once. I'm impressed. Thank you, son. I'll talk to you soon."

Okay, she threw in a little zinger at the end there. Probably couldn't resist. I hung up.

"Everything all right?" asked Roxie, sitting down next to me on the bed.

"Yeah," I said, still puzzled over the contents of the call.

"Who was it?"

"My mom."

"Did she like the mantilla?" Aha. One mystery solved. Now, if I could only figure out who killed Matt, I'd be one kick-ass detective.

"Very much. How'd you manage that, Roxie?"

"The second day I picked you up, you asked me to remind you you needed to shop for a birthday present for your mom. But you've been kind of preoccupied, so I took care of it."

"How'd you know where to send it?"

"I'm an enterprising girl. You mentioned the town she lives in. Took about two minutes to track her down."

"Well, whatever a mantilla is, she liked it a hell of a lot more than anything I ever bought her."

"It's a Mexican prayer shawl. Beautifully embroidered. Black. Just so you can sound like you know what you're talking about next time you speak to her."

I smiled. "Would have never thought of that myself, but it was a big hit."

"You said she was a black belt Catholic. I figured if there's anything those Mexicans know, it's all that Catholic mumbo jumbo."

A man more devout than I might have been offended by Roxie's religious dig. But it went right over my head. I was inured. You spend a few hundred hours in AA rooms and you'll hear more Catholic bashing than you would at a lifetime of Ku Klux Klan rallies. The majority of the people at 12-step meetings are recovering Catholics, too.

"Well, thank you. I really appreciate it."

"You're welcome," she said softly. I was intensely aware of how close Roxie was to me, of the hypnotic pattern of blue shading in her irises, of the flush on her cheeks, of her parted lips. Those lips.

The blood in my head felt like it was swirling, suspending all thought. I leaned in toward Roxie and she tilted her mouth up toward mine, closing her eyes.

Then the phone rang, jolting me upright. Reality, as usual, arrived with a rush of guilt, one strong enough to make me wince. They were paying me to find a murderer, not romance one of their employees. If I wanted to craft a tombstone that truly reflected my time on this planet, it would probably read, "What was I thinking?"

Roxie hadn't reacted at all to the phone. Her eyes were

still closed. Her mouth waiting for mine. "Umm, I better get that," I said

Her hand came up to her collar. She looked at me with an expression of hurt and astonishment. Good work, McNamara; now both of you feel bad.

"Hello," I said, spearing the receiver.

"Jim, it's Whitey. I'm at a copy shop in Venice Beach. The guy says the fax is theirs. But he was a little puzzled because they're not open at the hour it was sent. The guy who was working last night could have set it for timed delivery at the customer's request. But he's not here and he isn't answering his home phone."

"All right, Whitey. How are you going to leave it?"

"I left a message for the night guy to call me. I have some personal errands to run. I'll see you after the show tonight."

"All right, Hoss. See you then."

Roxie had stood up and was over at the window, taking in my unremarkable view, a frown on her face.

I wanted her and I think the attraction was mutual. But as you may have inferred, I'm not the most stable guy on campus. As they say in AA, alcoholics don't have relationships; they take hostages. I spent my whole life rushing into things and I have the stitches to prove it.

So I felt like before we got more deeply involved, a brief talk was in order about what were reasonable expectations. A little advance warning is only fair. When someone invites you over for dinner, you don't wait until you get there to inform them you're a strict vegan.

"Would you like to catch some lunch, Roxie?"

"No, thanks. I better get back to the office," she said, gathering her things. "The day of the results show is always hectic. I'm sure today is extra insane."

"Okay. Are you going to pick me up before the show?"

"Why don't we meet over there?" she asked, pulling the strap of her bag over her shoulder and turning at the door to look at me with a heartbreakingly neutral expression.

I nodded and she left. Another satisfied customer.

Whitey's call reminded me of something. I flipped through the phone book, looking for the number for Slice of Heaven pizza. I could have just dialed information and been connected. Tootsi Frootsi was paying my expenses, so I didn't need to be frugal. But old habits die hard.

"Is Don there?" I asked when a guy answered.

"Not until five," he said. "He comes in for the dinner rush."

That was precisely the time the *Star Maker* broadcast started. The delivery guy would have to wait.

I put on some workout gear and walked down the street to a Bally gym I had seen. A guy who looked like Jack LaLanne's bastard son in a tight black Lacoste shirt eventually sold me a day pass after the usual argument about how it would definitely behoove me to buy a lifetime membership instead.

I went in the weight room, stretched for a while and then threw iron until my blood was knocking like radiators in an old house and I was panting for breath. Then I went to the exhibitionists' parlor—the cardio room paneled with mirrors—and stormed a Stairmaster until I was spritzing like a six-foot-two rain cloud. I wiped down the machine and went back to the hotel to shower.

Afterward I grabbed a cheeseburger over at the market and made the lonely walk up to the studio. It was nearly as long a distance inside the compound to the *Star Maker* theater as it was getting to the gate. A couple of guys who whizzed by me in their golf carts seemed to be in homicidal moods.

This was my first results show and the air was charged.

Although it was the beginning of the season, the singers already had their own passionate cheering sections, waving handmade placards. "We Flip for Flip," read one. "Neveah Is Almost Heaven" insisted another. The crowd didn't require any encouragement this night.

I stood in the same spot and Roxie materialized just as the theme song began, bumping against me by way of hello. We looked at each other and both smiled.

Compared to the previous day's marathon, the half-hour live show was over in a flash. Rodney, who had bounced out a side door countless times the day before to smoke his menthol cigarettes, stayed in his seat the entire time.

Brian Breeze came out and introduced the judges. L.A. rolled his fist above his head as the crowd chanted, "Coop, Coop." Sugar Kane batted her eyes coquettishly at the camera, tapping at a wad of surgical gauze affixed to her neck.

After the crowd booed Rodney, Breeze announced, "Out of more than fifty thousand singers who auditioned for this year's show, these are your ten finalists, America."

The camera dollied across ten faces. All but Shontika were smiling.

"After last night's show, we received a record number of votes," he went on. I thought that was a clever way to finesse the low totals. "But someone must go home tonight. The results may shock you. But if your favorite doesn't advance, you have no one to blame but yourself. Remember: You *have* to vote, America. It's completely up to you."

Another nice touch, I thought. Put the onus on the viewers.

The singers sat in two rows of folding chairs stage right, ten yards in front of where Roxie and I stood. Breeze would render verdict on them one at a time. "JoJo, you sang 'Stuck With You.' L.A. said you 'got your groove on.' Sugar said you were 'absolutely delightful.' And Rodney called it 'aggressively noxious.' America's voted, JoJo and you...are safe. Stay right where you are."

Or "Neveah, you sang 'If This Is It.' L.A. said he's heard you better. Sugar said you were 'the bomb' and Rodney said if you made it through to next week, 'it would be a travesty.' America voted, Neveah....Come and stand with me."

By the end of the half hour, he had separated Greg, Neveah and Shontika from the rest of the herd. When he told Shontika to join him, the crowd gasped.

There was a smattering of boos when he revealed at the end she was going home. Shontika stood next to Breeze , stone-faced, as he cheerily declaimed, "Call me the Breeze." Then she was mobbed by the nine survivors, who came over to hug and commiserate. Eva, who was Shontika's main antagonist, could barely contain her grief, big crocodile tears running down her face. It was a phonier display of emotion than you'll ever see at a beauty contest.

Then it was over. The crowd began to disperse, except for the families of the singers, who made their way up onto the stage. Down in the front row, I saw L. A. Cooper in close consultation with a square-faced guy with a blond ponytail and a tangerine dress shirt with an enormous open collar.

I saw their hands come together in a quick transfer. It was a covert exchange I recognized immediately because I had participated in it a thousand times when I scored drugs.

"Who's that guy?" I asked Roxie. She looked over at Cooper and his friend, who were exchanging parting pleasantries. She scrunched up her face. "I've seen him around a lot, but I don't know his name. Hold on." She consulted briefly with the stage manager, a young woman wearing a headset. Roxie nodded several times as the stage manager spoke into her ear.

Then Roxie walked back over, frowning. "His name's Bumper Carlson," she said. "Apparently he's a big dealer. Sells roofies, pot, Ecstasy, coke—whatever you need—to a lot of people on the set. Including, as we just saw, one of the judges. How naïve am I that this guy's been selling drugs all this time right under my nose and I never knew it?"

"People like him generally like to keep a low profile," I said. "Let's see if we can flush him out into the light."

Cooper had taken the steps and was crossing the stage in front of us. "Hey, L.A.," I called out. He turned, smiling automatically at being hailed on his home turf. The smile faded when he realized he didn't know me. "How's it going?" I asked.

He flicked his chin at me.

"L.A.?" Roxie interceded. "This is Jim McNamara. He's the one looking into Matt's situation?"

"Oh, yeah, all right, duck. I got you." He came over affably, offering his hand. He looked big on television, but up close in person he had a density and a forward pitch to his posture that was menacing. "So how's that going? You getting anywhere?"

"Making steady progress," I said. "Listen, what's the deal with you and Bumper?"

Like a folding knife, his expression snapped into one of hostility.

"Say what?"

"I'm wondering what your tastes run to in recreational drugs."

He took an intimidating step up to me, rolling his shoulder. "The fuck you think you're talking to?"

"Oh, don't be modest," came a voice over my shoulder.

Rodney, still wearing the black muscle shirt he always did on the air, had approached from backstage and was standing beside Roxie. "Coop here is one of Mr. Carlson's best customers. This man goes through more date rape powder than your average Arab sultanate."

L.A. wheeled to face the attack on his flank. "Fuck you, Rodney. You keep your smart mouth shut or I'll shut it for you."

"You met our lawyers, Jerry and Richard, this morning, Mr. McNamara," continued Hampden, looking up defiantly at Cooper. "Did you know they spend most of their time trying to squash lawsuits brought by poor girls who have fallen under Coop's chemical spells? All these hopeful young ladies come out here for a shot at fame, little realizing that they have enlisted in Mr. Cooper's harem."

"You little asshole," said Cooper, cocking his fist and gathering himself to charge. Rodney's blond assistant, who I realized at that moment looked like Tiger Woods's bride, stepped in front of her boss and began pushing him away, toward the lip of the stage.

"How many this season, Coop?" called out Hampden as he was being backpedaled. "How many girls took you up on your kind offer of after-hours advice?"

Rodney's aide-de-camp turned him and pushed him down the steps. L.A. stood there fuming. Then he windmilled his arm, spluttered, "Fuck y'all," and stormed toward the rehearsal space.

I looked around the empty theater. The raised voices had cleared the area of people as effectively as a neutron bomb. I looked at Roxie and winked. "Now we're making progress."

CHAPTER 20

A flurry of activity followed every results show. Roxie stuck around to help the local Fox affiliates across the country tape their specious behind-the-scenes-at-*Star-Maker* segments for the late news.

As I walked out into the parking lot, a voice accosted me from the bushes. I figured maybe it was a rival roofies dealer trying to pick off the stragglers Bumper had missed. But it was Rodney, smoking a cigarette in the shadows.

"'Scuse me, mate. Could I have a word?"

I walked over to him intrepidly. The fact was, standing in the dark puffing away, Rodney looked pretty fiendish, like a theme-park Dracula on his break.

"What's up?"

He regarded me intently, his thick eyebrows beetling. It felt oddly like being X-rayed. Maybe he was a vampire. "I'm sorry about sticking my nose in there with Cooper, but the man's stupidity infuriates me. This show is the biggest money machine in the business. It's going to make me a very, very wealthy man before all is said and done. And he threatens that every time he indulges in his craven perversion. It's a miracle it hasn't blown up in our faces already, but I assure you, *Star Maker* would not survive a scandal like that—one of the judges taking sexual advantage of these innocent young singers, many of them teenagers."

I nodded assent.

"I can see it on his face. Every year we go to six cities to audition thousands of these kids and I know exactly what's he's thinking when a certain type of girl walks in the room. And it has nothing to do with her vocal range. It's: 'She would look great passed out naked underneath me.' He's a fucking idiot and he's pissing away the best thing that ever happened to him. I thought if I could embarrass him in public in there, it might make him see the light. But he's bloody hopeless."

"My main concern is finding out who killed Matt," I said. "As you know, he was sedated with Rophynol before he was strangled. So I was working my way back to the dealer who sells a lot of that drug. Unless you think Cooper might have been involved?"

"With Matt?" asked Rodney with some astonishment. "As far as I know he's only interested in raping unconscious girls, but who knows? One insensate body is much like another, I would imagine." He took a deep inhale on his cigarette. "Speaking of Matt's death, I don't know if this has occurred to you, but it seems quite possible to me that whoever killed him is the same person flogging Shontika's criminal past. In other words, someone is attempting to manipulate the results. And that I cannot allow."

Rodney pointed his cigarette at me to emphasize this point. The gesture looked like he was playing darts in a pub. "It's hard enough to package one of these rank amateurs as a star when the most talented one actually prevails. I can make the best of a bad lot. But if someone is trying to fix the race..." He pursed his lips disapprovingly, shaking his head.

"I'm proceeding with that in mind—that the two events could well be connected," I said.

"See that you do," he said, disengaging from me utterly and instantly the way only egomaniacs can. One second we were talking; the next I didn't exist.

Rodney flipped the cigarette away and walked toward the curb. A liveried chauffeur sprang from the gleaming black sedan parked there and hustled around to open the rear door. "This show has weathered a number of challenges, but if people thought the winner could be fixed, that would be the end of it. Game over.

"Not that I care," he added nonchalantly. "I've had quite enough of being in the limelight, thank you. But if *Star Maker* went down in flames, it would just about kill poor Ian." He slid into the back of his Maybach and the chauffeur shut the door.

Rodney's concern for others was so touching, I thought as I walked back to my hotel. Oh, and thanks for offering me a lift.

Sitting on my bed, I tried calling my sponsor, Chris. When my mind was a rat's nest as it was that night, he could usually help me untangle it. But he wasn't home.

I turned on the TV. It's different watching in Los Angeles. As Yogi Berra would say, "It gets late early out there." *SportsCenter* was on. The Lady Huskies were on a tear. The clips showed them schooling B.C. Fast-break city.

I fell asleep with the set still on. Goodnight, Conan, my sweet prince.

The next morning, I was waiting for Whitey outside the

lobby, freshly scrubbed. We had agreed to meet for the same early-bird meeting. Patsy's dad, Lenny, was there again, skulking back in the kitchen. He averted his eyes when I drifted in for some bad coffee.

The waffles afterward more than made up for it. I'm a pancake, not a waffle guy, so I'm not really qualified to say whether they were all-Pacific. But they were awesome.

Back at the hotel, there was a message from my sponsor saying he would be at home until noon Pacific time. I called right away.

"Hey, Chris," I said when he answered.

"Hey, Jim. How's it going?" I heard him suppressing a yawn.

"Tired?"

"I'm not sleeping well lately. I keep waking up in the middle of the night and then I can't get back to sleep."

"Uhh, I hate when that happens." I wasn't dissembling. Insomnia is like torture to me. All those empty, haunted hours.

"I'm okay with it," Chris said. "I see it as a chance to catch up on my prayers. So when I wake up, I hit my knees. The time seems to pass smoothly."

"You could try watching *Star Maker*. That would put you right out."

"I did watch it last night. I had the late shift at the rehab and the kids were all gathered in the TV lounge. I take it that was a big upset when Shontika was let go?"

"You have no idea," I replied. I brought Chris up to speed on all the intrigue at the show, the threat to reveal Shontika's criminal past, Eva's speed-freak friends, the popularity of date-rape drug at the set and my conversation with Rodney.

"So what's your theory, Quincy?" he asked. The reference to Jack Klugman as a crime-solving coroner was a pet name he had given me years ago, before I became a detective.

"I don't know. It's hard to rule any of them out, except maybe Patsy. She's too sweet. I can't see her hurting anyone. And Greg has a solid alibi. Eva has certainly come way up on the odds board. The thing is, *Star Maker* is the biggest thing that will ever happen to these kids. Win and you have a glamorous and lucrative singing career. Come in second or third or fourth and you're a trivia answer."

"Well, I'm certainly no expert on *Star Maker*," Chris responded. "But in the couple of times I've seen it, I have to say I really like Rodney. He's smug and pompous, but his comments are always perfectly honest. And that's such a novel quality on television." I chuckled in agreement.

"If Rodney is right," he continued, "and you seem to be leaning in this direction—then Matt's death was an attempt to fix the results."

"Yeah."

"Well, that puts whoever killed him on a treadmill. Because every week there's going to be a new threat you have to dispose of somehow."

"Right, and this week it was Shontika."

"But whoever is behind this must be going crazy. There's too many factors you can't control. First there's the performance. You hit a sour note one night—and these are amateur singers, so there's a good chance of that happening—and you're toast."

"Okay."

"So you'd have to be one of the elite singers to start with, someone with a good chance of winning on merit, otherwise week after week you'd have to kill or blackmail all the competition one by one just to stay in contention."

"I don't know. Having met these kids, Chris," I said,

"I have to tell you, I don't think there's one of them who doesn't think they deserve to win."

"Even so, it becomes like a game of Russian roulette because the viewer vote is quirky at best. Last night, all the girls at the rehab were cooing about Ricky. As soon as the show ended, they fanned out around the building to try to vote for him. And he might have been the worst of the pack."

"No argument there."

"Say you're convinced that big farm boy is your biggest threat—I think he's got a good voice by the way..."

"Cletus. Yeah. Me, too."

"So you try to eliminate him. Then the vote totals come in and Ricky's on top. You just killed the wrong person."

"Unless you wait until after the results show."

"And how many weeks you think you could get away with killing the frontrunner before all these kids were put in the singer protection program and delivered to the studio in armored cars?"

"Yeah, the producers are getting pretty frantic about their product being tampered with," I said. "They're very close to going into bunker mode."

"Personally, if I was trying to pull this off," said Chris, "I think your best chance to fix the results on *Star Maker* would be to get to that woman who picks the songs."

"Sandy Bauer?"

"Yeah. She has more influence on the results than anyone. You want someone out? Give them a bad song, or one that doesn't fit their range. Or during the week, just miscoach them so they sound stupid. This material all seems to date from before these kids' times, so a savvy person could misdirect them and they'd never know. Until they saw Rodney wincing."

As we chatted, I admitted the case was stressing me

because with each day, the list of possible perpetrators seemed to be expanding rather than shrinking.

"I don't want to add to your misery, but there's a possibility that keeps pinching me," said Chris. "What if Matt's death had nothing to do with fixing the *Star Maker* results? What if there was another motive altogether?"

"Oh, you're a big help."

"Sorry. What I would recommend, if all this is crowding your mind, is to step away from it for a day. Let your subconscious work on it."

That notion, it struck me, was so counterintuitive, it just might work. But first I had some detective work to do.

CHAPTER
21

I called Roxie, who picked me up and drove me over to the studio where the *Star Maker* contestants were making their song selections for the next show.

Everyone was gathered in the rehearsal space, divvying up the Glen Campbell catalogue. Suddenly Huey Lewis was starting to sound very hip indeed.

The mood of Sandy and the singers was sour and nervous. It didn't help that Rodney was pacing back and forth along the far wall like a tiger in a zoo cage. As soon as a song began, he would punctuate his circuit by biting on his knuckle, smacking his forehead and cursing explosively to himself.

His furor was warranted. To hear Flip take a stab at "Southern Nights" or JoJo attempt to warble "By the Time I Get to Phoenix" was excruciating. The only decent vocal I heard that day was Cletus on "Galveston." He sang it about an octave deeper than Campbell had. Turns out the kid was a natural country singer in the vein of Randy Travis. Even Rodney stopped doing laps when Cletus sang. But the pacing resumed faster than ever when Eva followed that with her off-key mauling of "Rhinestone Cowboy."

"Is this Rodney's idea of providing encouragement?" I asked.

"I don't know what he's doing here," said Roxie. "He's never attended one of these song-selection sessions before. He must be worried. He's been pulling out all the stops. He's flying over some childhood friend who's supposed to be some sort of good-luck charm. And he's bringing back Terry Taylor for a command performance next week. Rodney always says the show peaked in the second season, the year Terry won. I guess he thinks having Mr. *Star Maker* here will give the show a shot in the arm."

We listened patiently for a while, but when Neveah started butchering "I Wanna Live," I could take no more.

"Be right back," I whispered to Roxie, and headed toward the rehearsal space to look for Bobby. Just as I reached the door, Rodney executed an abrupt about face in midstride and I nearly bowled him over.

"Jesus," he said bitterly, "would you please put me out of my misery, Macca?"

"Macca? I thought that was Paul McCartney's nickname."

"It's what we call all you Paddys whose names start with an *M-C*."

"You mean all this time 'Macca' was actually an insult to Paul?"

"Not bloody likely. When you're as rich as that one, everything is a compliment."

"Too bad you couldn't use his songs on the show, huh?"

"This is insufferable, isn't it? I'm really at the end of my rope. What would you do, McNamara?"

"Pull a van Gogh."

"You mean cut off my ears?" he asked. It was the first time I had ever seen the corners of his mouth turn up. Now I knew why he didn't smile. It made him look demented, like a ravenous badger. "It may well come to that. But I meant about securing better material."

"As far as I'm concerned, there are only two certifiable pop geniuses in the current era: Jeff Lynne and Mutt Lange."

"You're kidding," he said, looking at me with surprise. "You wouldn't include Elton John or Paul Simon?"

"Not for my money. I might put Burt Bacharach in the category, but you have to be a special singer to do justice to his songs."

"Well, you're right about Lynne. We should definitely work up an Electric Light Orchestra theme night. Those songs are brilliant. But Lange? Why him?"

"Because he's a miracle worker. He could take a crappy headbanger band like Def Leppard or Loverboy and make them sound absolutely sublime. He turned a mediocre lounge singer, Shania Twain, into the best-selling country star of all time. Pop music is all about hooks and Mutt makes the sharpest I've ever heard."

He pursed his lips and tipped his head, an expression that said, *There is much in what you say, camel-breath.* Then he clapped his ears and cursed, "Oh, fuck me!"

Ricky Tavares had started singing "Gentle on My Mind." Rodney staggered off in agony.

Bobby was nowhere to be found. I returned to my seat and asked Roxie to call me a cab. "I'll drive you anywhere you want to go," she said.

"Not this time," I said. "This is an errand I need to run myself."

She shrugged, picked up her cell and walked off toward the theater to make a call. A minute later she was back "All set, Cappy," she said. "Your chariot awaits."

"Thanks," I said rising.

Putting her hands on my shoulders, Roxie went up on her tiptoes to whisper in my ear, in the process pressing the length of her body against me. "I have to go to a promotional shoot for the affiliates this afternoon. But I was hoping to come over to your hotel later tonight. Will you be there at ten?"

I nodded. Looking down into her sparkling eyes, I developed tunnel vision. The rest of the world disappeared. I was about to kiss her when she pushed away, settling back on her heels. "See you then," she said with a smile that made me—all props to Charlie Rich—glad that I'm a man.

I had retrieved the pizza guy Don Walmsley's address from the online White Pages. The taxi dropped me in front of his residence, a ramshackle three-story apartment building on the seedy fringes of West Hollywood. Don lived on the top floor. The balcony outside his door offered a view of a city bus yard and repair shed. The sound of air wrenches and tire machines filled the air. The noise was nerve-wracking, like an amplified dentist's office.

I knocked, setting off a noisy scramble on the other side of the door. A chunky guy with a puffy, pitted face and sparse hair answered. From the look of astonishment behind his black-framed bifocals, I surmised that Don didn't get many callers.

"Yeah?" he said. That came out squeaky. He coughed and tried again. "Yeah?" Better.

"Hi, my name's Jim McNamara. I'm a detective. Are

you Don?" He nodded. "May I ask you a few questions? It won't take long."

"What's this about?" he said suspiciously.

"It's an incident involving one of the contestants on *Star Maker.*"

"All I do is watch the show," he protested. "And I don't even get to do that all the time because I work nights. I'm saving up for TiVo."

I nodded. I could hear a TV commercial blaring in the room behind him.

"But you delivered to the hotel where the contestants stayed."

"Yeah," he said worriedly. After a moment of thought, he continued with relief, "But the guy I delivered to didn't make the finals. He left the show, I think."

"Right, first of all Don, you are completely in the clear. You're not accused of doing anything," I assured him. "I only wanted to ask you a few questions to verify someone else's testimony. It'll only take a second. May I come in?"

He scratched his head, offering a view of his armpit through the sleeve of a wrinkled bowling shirt. "I guess," he said, backing against the wall to let me in. I walked directly into the living room. There was a kitchenette to my right, and a bedroom beyond that. It smelled like Don was brewing a big batch of BO. I wondered how long I could hold my breath.

He gestured to a chair. Don resumed his place on the couch. I had interrupted his breakfast. He was eating Cinnamon Toast Crunch in an oversized yellow plastic bowl that looked like a dog had chewed on it. On the TV three feet in front of him, Ellen was interviewing Jennifer Love Hewitt. They seemed to be having a gay old time.

"Does the name *Matt Hanes* mean anything to you?"

He nodded his head. "It's not like I could tell you about every person I deliver a pizza to, but that guy was a regular. So yeah."

"Do you remember the last pizza you delivered to him at the hotel?"

He shook his head vigorously. "Yeah, but I never saw what's-his-name, Matt."

"What happened?"

"I pull up to the hotel. Like I say, he ordered from us every night for a while there. So I go through the lobby and get in the elevator, punch the button for the tenth floor and this guy jumps on just before the doors close. He's holding a big bottle of soda. It was green. I think it was Sierra Mist."

I nodded like this was important information.

"He looks at the pizza and says to me, 'Is that for 1022?' And I nod. He says, 'That's where I'm going. To Matt's room. We're watching the Lakers game. I'll save you the trip.' And he whips out a twenty and says, 'Keep it.'

"It seemed okay to me. I mean, he knew the guy's name and room number and he had the soda and all. Plus he was giving me a big tip. So I hand him the pizza and he thanks me and gets off at ten and I take the elevator back to the lobby. I never gave it a second thought."

"What did he look like, the guy in the elevator?"

"I don't know," he said, looking at me blankly. "Just a guy."

"Had you ever seen him before?"

"I don't know."

"Big? Small? Young? Old?"

"Average, I'd say."

"Do you remember what he was wearing?"

"Blue windbreaker and a Universal Studios cap. I deliver to a lot of hotels to tourists who are in town for *The*

Price Is Right. He looked like one of those people. Kinda average."

"Was he younger or older than the guy Matt who usually got the pizza?"

Don thought about this hard, looking up at the ceiling and folding in his lips. "Older?"

I might have continued to beat this dead horse, but it smelled like it was decomposing. "Okay," I said briskly, slapping my knees and standing up. "Thanks for your cooperation. I'll be going now."

He waved with one hand and resumed eating with the other. As I made for the door, he called out to me through a baffle of soggy cereal, "Hey, Detective?"

"Yeah, Don?"

"Do you like Ellen?"

"Sure."

He nodded, turning back to the set. "She's my favorite." He grabbed the remote and turned up the volume.

I had to walk about a mile before chancing upon a cab dropping off a fare. I had given up on hailing one. In that neighborhood there were more laundromats than there were taxis.

Back at the Farmer's Daughter, Whitey was parked in a space facing the portico. The side windows were tinted too dark to see through, but I spotted him through the windshield. He didn't notice me walk up to the driver's-side window, so absorbed was he in filling in the last few squares in the *L.A. Times* crossword puzzle.

"Hey," I said. Whitey didn't startle. He glanced over at me and kept writing.

"Hey," he replied.

"Everything all right?"

"Other than the fact that I just spent the morning chasing my tail?"

"You want to tell me about it inside or are you not getting out of your car today?"

"You know the name of a seven-letter estuary in Poland?"

"Not off the top of my head."

He tossed the paper onto the passenger seat and opened the door.

I let him stew in his juices on the way to my room, then asked, "Why so grumpy?"

"You know the clerk from the copy store?"

"Yeah?"

"He never returned my call. So I called his boss. The guy didn't show up for work last night. No call, no nothing. And the owner said he was his most responsible employee. So I went over and took a peek inside his apartment. All his stuff's there. No sign of foul play. His answering machine's still picking up calls, but he's gone. His neighbor said she hasn't seen him in a couple of days."

"Could be a spur-of-the-moment jaunt down to Mexico," I suggested hopefully.

"Or it could be whoever got him to send that fax took him out afterward."

"I don't know, Whitey. That seems awfully heavy-handed."

"Look, there must be fifty ways to send a traceless fax. But all that occurred to this person was the least anonymous way—using a clerk in a store. So we know he's an idiot. And stupid and violent often go together. Maybe he wanted to make sure this clerk could never identify him. The guy's body will probably wash up in a marina next week."

"You're assuming the worst. There are a ton of reasons why a guy would suddenly stop showing up for a McJob. Like he was bored. Or he got another offer closer to his house. Or he decided to visit a friend in Santa Cruz."

"Except the owner said he was completely steady."

I turned my hands up in submission. "I still don't understand why you're so pissy. Even if it went down the way you think, there's nothing you could have done to stop it."

"Yeah, but I should have followed this up more aggressively, not waited for the guy to call me. Now nearly forty hours have gone by. The trail is cold," he said, scowling.

"Whitey, we're not exactly the FBI. It's just you and me. No resources, no lab technicians, no field agents. We have the same chance of tracking down a missing person an hour or a month after they disappear. And if they don't want to be found, that chance is pretty small. Why don't we err on the sunny side and assume this guy is sitting in a bar in La Jolla right now, sipping a beer and thinking: I should have quit that crappy job six months ago."

That prospect made Whitey smile, maybe because it would be the typical alcoholic's reaction. "You're right. I'm taking this way too seriously."

"When I get wound up in a case, I remind myself, a detective is like a member of Al-Anon: I didn't cause it, I can't control it and I can't cure it."

His face softened a little more. "Hey, Whitey," I continued, turning my back to boot up my computer and check my e-mail. "You know I really value your help, but I keep wondering: How can you devote so much time to working with me and then not cash the checks? What are you—independently wealthy?"

"In a manner of speaking," he said. I glanced back. He was stretched out on the couch like Cleopatra's cat, his hand cupping his ear, a forearm bracing his head. "But it's a long, sorry story without a hero."

"Still like to hear it," I said, typing sporadically. I figured he might be more comfortable if I wasn't facing him.

That's how confessionals and therapy couches work, isn't it? You're not looking into anyone's eyes.

"Did I ever mention I'm third-generation Californian? Well, this really and truly is a California story, which means it involves cars. My father served in the Navy during the Korean War. I was conceived during a shore leave. He came home with a good trade, welding, and settled with my mom in Fresno.

"He had a couple of classic roadsters that he loved to work on and race. He also had a Shelby Mustang that he drove on weekends. My mom had a Buick station wagon as big as an aircraft carrier. But my dad drove this beater Ford Pinto to and from work. One night he stopped at an intersection on the way home and got rear-ended by a semi. His car was engulfed in flames and he burned to death.

"My mom had lawyers descend on her like sports agents on a Heisman Trophy winner. She picked a real sharpie out of Sacramento. He won her a fortune from the trucking company and a king's ransom from Ford for its design flaw. That settlement is still a record. You can look it up.

"The lawyers from Ford tried to point out that my dad had stopped at a bar for three hours after his shift was over. Mom's lawyer would have none of that. This was a hard-working, responsible man, a veteran and a loving husband and father. He wasn't going to let these buzzards from Detroit smear that reputation. Back in those days, you could still make that argument—that there was no shame to a man having a few drinks after a hard day's work

"The fact is, my dad was a full-blown alcoholic. He was probably three sheets to the wind when the truck hit him. He was most nights. But that doesn't mean it was his fault. Especially since the trucker had just driven straight through from Pittsburgh and was cross-eyed on black beauties."

I had stopped all pretense of typing and instead was staring out the window as Whitey told his story.

"My mom took the money and decided to move up valley to Colusa, where she was from. I was staying with my uncle, her brother, while she got resettled. The day of the move she was following the moving truck in her Buick. It was real foggy that morning out on Highway 5. The truck had to slam on its brakes to avoid a five-car pileup. I guess my mom never saw the brake lights. She hit the back of the truck doing sixty.

"They used the Jaws of Life to pry her out of the front seat. She was still alive when they put her in the ambulance, but she died on the way to the hospital. If you're partial to irony, she died in the exact reverse fashion of my father.

"So that left me, an eighteen-year-old hell-raiser, with more money than God. I drifted down to L.A. and spent the next six years drinking and drugging myself into a stupor. High times, Jim. I was living like I imagined Elvis would if he wasn't so damned concerned with taking care of business. You want to chase oblivion, this is the place to do it.

"I was leaving an after-hours club one morning in my Stingray when I hit this kid. That's what they told me, anyway. I was in a blackout. Nineteen years old. Just moved here with his family from the Philippines. He was crossing Ventura Boulevard to catch the first of three buses he took to go to classes at a JC.

"I was convicted of vehicular homicide, driving while impaired, and I think reckless endangerment. I remember my lawyer whistling when he saw my blood alcohol level at the time of my arrest. You've heard me share my AA story, so you know I found the program in prison.

"I gave most of my inheritance to that kid's family. They've done very well with it, investing in real estate in Orange County. I also established a scholarship in his name at the junior college he attended. Take it from someone who tried, though, you can't pay down guilt.

"When I got out, I met a guy in the rooms who was a financial genius. He belonged to the Warren Buffett school of investing: Buy and hold. He put me into Wal-Mart and Microsoft with the money I had left. Which is why I don't need to cash your checks. I live better than I deserve to on my dividends."

Whitey sat up. "Here's the final irony. The guy who set me up? He was a sharp stock evaluator, just like Bill Wilson, the patron saint of AA. Except, he went back out after seven months. Drank himself to death."

For the first time since he had started talking, we reestablished eye contact. I guess my feelings were written on my face.

"You look like you could use some cheering up," Whitey said. "I know a good Happy Hour meeting."

Whitey ran into some people he knew at the meeting and we all went out for a long, raucous dinner after. Slamming down the iced tea and swapping stories.

It was around nine-thirty when he dropped me back at the Farmer's Daughter. I hadn't been in my room long when there was a knock at the door. Thinking it was Roxie, I threw open the door, exclaiming, "Hello, gorgeous!"

JoJo Johnson looked up at me with an amused smile. Her blond hair was piled up in an artfully messy knot that showed off her creamy neck. She had on a red satin blouse, painted-on jeans and black pumps.

"I bet you say that to all the girls," she said.

I pulled back in surprise. "Sorry, I was..." I looked out in the hall past her to see if any of the other contestants were with her because her visit was so unexpected.

"May I come in?" she asked coquettishly.

"Sure," I said, gesturing her into the room. "What can I do for you, JoJo?"

She was surveying the space, her back to me. She half turned to respond. "You said any of us could come seek you out."

"Right," I said. At this point I had gotten over my surprise. "You have some information about Matt?"

JoJo looked pensive, as if she were pondering this. "I don't know," she said. "I'm just fascinated by what you do." She swished over to the couch that Whitey had recently lain on, sitting down in a curled-up sideways posture. "I thought you could tell me a little about how you work." She patted the other cushion invitingly.

I followed her over and sat. Let me make it clear: I knew she was working me. But I was enjoying watching her technique. If I were in some bizarro Hitchcock movie with Grace Kelly playing the villain instead of the victim, I'd willingly let her lead me to my doom just for the pleasure of seeing her operate.

"So how are you doing with Matt's murder?" she asked. "Any promising leads?" She opened her blue eyes wide and locked them on mine imploringly. It was like getting hit with a shot of sodium Pentothal. I would have told her my bank PIN if she asked. But not state secrets.

"Just stumbling along," I said. "You have any information that might help?"

"Me?" She fanned one manicured hand and touched it lightly to her chest. With her other hand, she pressed on my thigh. "I probably know less than anyone. But you know what I was wondering?" She put both hands demurely in her lap. "Who's that guy who works with you? You haven't introduced him."

"I'm not sure who you mean," I said, feigning inno-

cence. Whitey, after all, had gone to considerable lengths
not to let any of the contestants see us together.

"You know. Your pal. Looks like a big friendly bear.
Drives an SUV."

What she had told me was that we were under surveil-
lance by someone outside the *Star Maker* circle. And my
continued denial of Whitey told her that I was on to her.
She narrowed her eyes and plunged ahead. "Shontika told
us she got thrown off because of some fax. Do you know
where that came from?"

"No, I hit a dead end on that."

There was a long moment while we appraised each
other, pondering the significance of each other's lies. Then
she smiled, her cheeks dimpling. "You know I find you
very attractive," she said, putting one arm along the top
of the couch. Okay, she was going to take the seduction
route. JoJo obviously had a limited repertoire, but she was
a gamer. You have to admire that. I had her on a short
leash, but before she could even get started there was a
knock at the door.

I got up to answer it. Who was I expecting? To be honest, I thought it might be JoJo's pimp who would burst into
the room indignantly to pull the old Beauty and the Beast
shakedown routine.

It was Roxie. "Hey, Cappy," she said with a radiant
smile. She had her hair pulled back in a ponytail. She was
wearing a short-sleeve sweater, robin's-egg blue, and a
white-lace peasant dress. She looked beautiful.

She walked into the room, fanning a plastic clamshell.
"I brought one of my favorite DVDs. It's…" She stopped in
midsentence and midstride, having spotted my visitor, who
had rearranged herself more suggestively on the couch.

"Roxie!" cried out JoJo, dangling a bare foot. "What a
surprise. You guys working late?"

Blushing a deep red, Roxie looked at me accusingly. "I have to go," she said, streaming for the door.

"Roxie, wait," I said. But she was past me and gone.

I took a few deep breaths through my nose, staring forlornly at the door.

"That was a little awkward, huh?" said JoJo.

"Let's cut the games, shall we?" I said, advancing angrily toward the couch. "Why don't you tell me who you're working for, JoJo?"

She laughed and began to languorously gather herself. She stood in front of me and chucked my chin. "Anyone who knows me, Mr. McNamara, will tell you that I've always been my own girl. See you around campus," she said, moving her tom-tom strut toward the door.

I considered trying to restrain her. But you need a lot more leverage than I had to turn a woman like that.

It was pretty obvious that Roxie wasn't returning my calls. Now, I'm not sure, but I think that's a clear-cut violation of the Hollywood assistant's oath.

But it seemed like a good opportunity to take my sponsor's advice and step away from the case for a day. Air my head out a little. So that next morning, I arranged for a rental car with the mayor of Hooterville—I mean the concierge at the Farmer's Daughter—and drove to San Bernardino National Park north of Rancho Cucamonga.

Hiking is my favorite recreation. Funiculee, funicula. There's something about traipsing over hill and dale that I find intensely satisfying. Most of my goals in life are pretty short-term—like making it to lunch. But someday I'd like to walk the length of the Appalachian Trail, from Georgia to Maine.

It takes a few miles to find the bliss in hiking. I guess you have to tire the body out first. But eventually you enter into a transcendent state, where you're existing purely in the moment. Moving through nature, enjoying the spectacle and breathing the oxygenated air. All the hectoring thoughts that seem to ricochet around your head just vanish.

At least that's how it is for me. San Bernardino was perfect. Steep climbs, gorgeous vistas and precious few people around. It strikes me that may be why I like hiking so much—the isolation. I really savor my time alone.

All day long I focused on keeping my mind clear, just putting one foot in front of the other. I reserved the long ride back to the city to think about *Star Maker*.

To wit: It was obvious from JoJo's command performance at my hotel that she was involved in the attempt, by any means necessary, to fix the *Star Maker* results. But she didn't seem either smart or ambitious enough to be pulling the strings. And her whereabouts were accounted for on the night Matt was murdered.

I thought about what my sponsor Chris had said: that backing one horse in this race, even if you were cheating, would be difficult to arrange successfully. There were just too many factors to control. But, it occurred to me, those odds got a lot better if you had two ringers among the contestants, especially one of each gender. Then even if the voting totals were unpredictable in a way that worked against you, you still had a player in the game. And both Whitey and Roxie had agreed that the results tended to get less volatile in the final five weeks of the show.

That left Bobby as the wild card. He was the one with the most to gain from the murder. Matt completely overshadowed Bobby. As long as he was in the competition, Bobby didn't stand a chance. With him gone, Bobby was an instant frontrunner. More importantly, Bobby was the only one still without an alibi. I was determined to get that situation resolved.

Famished after my hike, I stopped essentially on impulse at a California Pizza Kitchen on my way back to the hotel. It was surreal what I found on that menu. They've perverted the whole concept of pizza out there, designating ingredients like artichokes and broccoli as toppings.

You can cram stuff like that inside a pita sandwich. I don't know why you'd want to, but you could do it. But those items don't belong within a hundred miles of a pizza. It's the culinary equivalent of combining matter and antimatter.

Pizza is one of the staples of the American diet. It's a very simple formula: cheese, sauce, crust. Meat toppings are optional. Your choices from the vegetable kingdom are restricted to mushrooms, olives and onions. Any attempt to make this dish more exotic is destined to be an abomination.

I made it through most of my plain pie, trying to ignore the fact that it tasted rather florid. As I chewed, I considered other options. So far I had JoJo and Bobby on the dark side. But I didn't know if they were working in tandem. And there were others involved in this deadly scam as well. Someone had clearly been spying on me, or else JoJo wouldn't have been fishing around for Whitey's identity.

What I didn't have a handle on was who was in charge of this conspiracy. I needed to squeeze the pieces that were on the board, see what they revealed.

I spent a restless night in my hotel room. Still no messages from Roxie. I made a fitful attempt to watch TV, flipping through the channels several times without sticking. With the remote in my hand, I felt like a kid glumly riding a rinky merry-go-round I was far too big for.

My legs were achy from the hike. I thought longingly of Harmony, the ultra-masseuse back in Connecticut. I settled for a couple of ibuprofen liqui-gels and read a paperback of Joseph O'Connor's, *Star of the Sea,* for forty minutes before falling asleep.

In the morning I had breakfast at the Farmers Market, spent a painful fifteen minutes riding a stationary bike in the hotel gym to work the kinks out of my legs and drove over to the Star house. Without Roxie, my chauffeuse, I was getting good use out of my rental car. I was surprised at how little trouble I had finding the house. I guess I had been paying more attention than I realized.

In the parking area, I saw Eva leaning in the window of a rented economy car, talking to her overweight, mono-chrome sister. I saw Eva's daughter strapped into a child's seat in the rear. The poor kid looked like she had been crying for days. Her little eyes were beet-red and pus was running from her lower lid.

Eva's sister passed her what looked like a baggy filled with used tissues. The punk girl patted the top of the car and they drove off. Eva and I approached the door to-gether.

"Your daughter all right?" I asked.

"She's fine. Just a little touch of pinkeye. She gets it all the time."

I nodded, wishing I had some helpful medical advice for the child. "Is everyone home?"

Eva brushed ahead of me to open the door. "Hell if I know. I ain't takin' attendance." The other girls—Neveah, JoJo and Patsy—were lounging in the sunken living-room area along with Ricky. Eva called out gaily, "All right, ladies, as promised, free makeovers this morning." She picked up what looked like a patent-leather hat box off the table by the couch. "Got my beauty kit right here. You wanna be up first, Neveah?"

"All right," said Neveah, shrugging. Eva waved her over and got her settled in a chair she placed before a mirror.

As I headed up the stairs to look for Bobby, I saw Eva take out the bag of crumpled tissues, unseal it and place it on her work table next to a package of facial wipes. Then, gabbing away happily, she set to work on Neveah's face.

I went right at the top of the stairs to the room I thought was Bobby's. Turning the knob, I saw a naked Clete on all fours on the bed, his feet facing the door, his head dangling between his shoulders. Behind him and pumping away strenuously, while grunting, "Yeah, baby," through clenched teeth was Flip. His naked butt cheeks were clenching and unclenching like fists with each thrust.

As I backed out of the room with my eyes squeezed shut, I was thinking how much I wished I hadn't seen that. It was a tableau that was going to be burned on my corneas for a long time—Flip struggling to do his business while staying atop the far larger man. It looked like a horny Chihuahua trying to mate with a Newfoundland.

I opened the door to the adjoining bedroom. "Who's there?" called out Bobby like a blind man, which I guess at the moment he was. He was sitting in front of a mirror, his springy hair tied back, a pair of orange plastic eyeshields fitted over his nose while he misted his face, neck and shoulders with a spray can of tanning solution.

"It's Jim McNamara."

"Ever hear of knocking, McNamara?" he said angrily.

After getting an eyeful of Flip and Clete, I was definitely regretting barging into rooms in this house. But I didn't feel like explaining that to Bobby.

"What the fuck do you want?" he asked, pinching the cover off his eyes as if he were removing a pince-nez.

"Came by to put you on notice, sport," I said. "You have until the results show in two days to produce the girl who was with you on the night of Matt's murder. Bring her to the studio. I want to talk to her face-to-face. If she's not there, that'll be the last *Star Maker* episode you appear on, Bobby. That is, assuming you don't get voted off Wednesday anyway."

"Fuck you, McNamara. You don't have the authority to kick anyone off. Especially not the voter favorite."

"If that girl isn't there on Wednesday, we'll find out, won't we?" I asked smirking. "You have a shiny, happy day, Bobby."

As I walked down the steps and out of the house, a fully made-up Neveah was sitting on the couch, singing harmony to an R. Kelly song with Ricky. An unadorned Patsy was talking to Greg by the kitchen door. And Eva, brandishing one of her tissues, was chasing after JoJo. "Get away from me, Eva," JoJo said, holding up an arm defensively. "How many times I have to tell you I don't want you doing my face?"

I was happy to flee to a larger and, I hoped, saner world. Whitey and I hooked up in the late afternoon, took in an attitude-adjustment meeting and then went to a Lakers game a friend had given him tickets to. Good tickets too. We were three rows back under the basket.

The Phil Jackson–Kobe Bryant reunion didn't seem to be going so well. A young Bulls team was running them off the court. But the people-watching courtside was fabulous.

You would have thought Whitey was Jack Nicholson by the number of people who came up to say hello before and during the game. As we made our way back to the car, he said, "So? When are you going to explain to me how you fucked it up with Roxie so bad?"

"You talk to her?"

"Uh, yeah."

"She's not answering any of my calls."

"Can you blame her? She shows up for a romantic evening and you're entertaining the *Star Maker* sex kitten? That wasn't real good planning."

"For God's sake, Whitey," I said exasperatedly. I told him about JoJo's drop-by visit, her keen interest in him, my deadline for Bobby and, reluctantly, about the passion of Clete and Flip.

"No shit," he replied, having less trouble than I did fitting that coupling into his worldview.

"Anyway, it's obvious that whoever is behind this knows we're working together," I said, "so starting with tomorrow's taping we can arrive and leave together."

Whitey nodded.

"So how long you think Roxie is going to stay mad at me?"

"Oh, I think she knows you weren't fooling around with JoJo. She just didn't like having to consider the possibility."

CHAPTER 25

Oh, what a taping it was. The nine *Star Maker* finalists doing Glen Campbell songs. It made artichokes on pizza look like a match made in heaven. I go pretty deep with the American songbook, and even I only recognized about four of the selections.

But it was worth it to watch Rodney suffer. It's a good thing they kept the camera off him during the performances because he was writhing in his seat as if he were in the final stages of some black plague. They had to shut his mic off because he kept moaning and cursing. At one point, when Stan Jacobs, the director, asked Ricky to do another take of "Gentle on My Mind," Rodney stood up, staring at the ceiling, and screamed, "If there is a God up there, strike me dead right now. I beg of you!" Then he ran out the exit door to smoke another cigarette.

This despite the fact that Rodney had all his good-luck charms in place. His childhood friend, George Oglesby, whom he had flown over from England, turned out to be a sweet, nearly bald, pie-faced man with rimless glasses.

And Terry Taylor was in the house. The second-season *Star Maker* winner showed up with a big, bitchy entourage just before noon. They closeted themselves in the matching giant trailers he had demanded be parked in the lot. Terry emerged only to lip-synch his latest single, "(You Make Me) Tingle."

In the segment that followed, he was graciousness itself to the finalists. Breeze asked him how he would advise these kids to handle the pressure of the show. "Drink heavily," he said with a straight face. Then he cracked up and the audience roared. "I'm kidding. I'm kidding. The thing is, none of you would be here if you weren't super, super talented. Just hold on to that. Work hard." He looked probingly into their eyes as he spoke. "You have to do the spadework. The rest of it will take care of itself. Above all, believe in yourself and savor this experience. Y'all are on the ride of your lives." He smiled radiantly.

The nine finalists applauded madly as if the Dalai Lama had just imparted the secret of life to them. The crowd gave Terry an ovation, which he acknowledged with his usual bashful head-bobbing.

Once the cameras were turned off it was another story. Neveah, who had been wearing oversized sunglasses all day, ran over to thank Terry and reached for his hand. He recoiled in horror. "Don't touch me, you cow."

Even that rank insult, which the entire studio audience heard, didn't keep the finalists from following Terry back to his trailer, hoping for an audience or maybe a blessing. This, after all, was the only guy in the history of the show who had parlayed a win on *Star Maker* into a viable singing career. They were hoping some of that mojo would rub off.

Terry stopped at the entrance to his double-wide and

turned back to address them. "Listen, here's the real deal. Y'all are a disgrace. I don't know who told any of you that you could sing, but they were lying. People are laughing at you. Do you get that? Not that it matters. This show is so over. First season, second season, it was a big deal. The winners those years—me and Jenny—have careers. But no one even remembers who won the third and fourth seasons. This well done run dry, boys and girls. You're just fighting over the dry dog shit at the bottom. Whether you get sent home this week or next week, you're all losers." With that, he gathered his embossed robe around him and flounced into the trailer. The robe, by the way, in case you missed the ubiquitous ads, was the signature piece in his new clothing line. Genuine Terry cloth, get it?

His tirade really deflated the singers. They returned to the stage looking shell-shocked. You haven't heard bad music until you've heard Glen Campbell tunes sung by teenagers who have just been sapped of all reason to live.

I watched the taping from my customary spot, just offstage standing next to Roxie. She had greeted me that morning with a shy wave. "I'm sorry I've been so fussy," she said, looking at my shoes in a penitent pose. "I'll make it up to you," she said, looking up and smiling. Whatever tension there was between us vanished. Whitey took up position at the back of the auditorium.

As the day ground along, there was a brief debate between Stan in the booth and Neveah onstage before she sang "I Wanna Live."

"You have to take them off, sweetheart," Stan insisted.

"Why? T-Beau got to wear sunglasses during half his performances last year," she objected. Roxie informed me she was standing on firm precedent. The previous season, T-Beau, a long-haired Southern "rocker," had worn hideous Anna Wintour–style goggles while singing most of his songs.

"And T-Beau, my dear," announced Stan over the speakers, "is back singing Lynyrd Skynyrd covers in Gulfport. Now take them off."

Reluctantly, she removed her sunglasses. It was immediately obvious why she had wanted to cover up. In fact, there were some gasps from the audience. Neveah looked like an alien. Her eyes were shockingly red and running.

Her voice, however, was better than I had ever heard it. There was an extraordinary plangent tone to it, as if her heart were breaking. And maybe it was.

The guy I was looking for didn't show up until late in the day. Dealers generally don't work the early shift. Just before Bobby wrapped up with "Witchita Lineman," a pretty good performance, by the way—relatively speaking—I noticed Bumper slip into the back of the hall. I also noticed Whitey, who I had alerted to watch for a guy with a blond ponytail, latch onto Bumper, making sure he didn't slip back out before we talked to him.

Once it was a wrap and the crowd began to disperse, Whitey and I shadowed Bumper at a discreet distance, watching him do his rounds. At one point, L. A. Cooper started in Bumper's direction, spotted us, glared and headed off backstage.

Bumper was apparently so comfortable plying his trade in the Larry Hagman Theater that he didn't notice us until we approached him as he sat splay-legged in the middle of the fifth row, waiting for customers.

"Hey, Bumper," I hailed him, sidling into his row. Even though he didn't recognize me, he offered me a lifted chin and an encouraging smile. Then he saw Whitey making his way over from the other aisle.

Bumper stopped smiling and held up his hands. "Hey, fellas," he said placatingly, "let's go easy, okay? I'm here by invitation."

"I'm sure you are," I said, as Whitey and I settled into the chairs on either side of him. Turning his head from one to the other of us, he looked like a spectator at a tennis match. "We only want to ask you a few questions. I'm Jim McNamara. I've been hired to look into the death of Matt Hanes. This is my associate Whitey Stahl."

He nodded at each of us. "Yeah, I heard you were around. I hope you don't think—"

"We don't think anything, Bumper," I interrupted him. "We have no interest in messing up your situation here. We just want the answers to a few questions. Talk to us honestly and we'll be out of your hair in two minutes."

"All right," he said, drawing the words out hesitantly.

"So, we know you sell roofies," I began. "No offense, but can you make a living off that?"

Probably not the most politic opening to a conversation, questioning a guy's livelihood, but I wanted to move him away from a knee-jerk denial as quickly as possible. Bumper tilted his head resignedly. "I'm more diversified than that. But that happens to be a very popular item in this town. L.A. is like a magnet for young innocent talent. Always has been."

I winced a little, knowing that when he referred to talent, it wasn't the acting variety he meant. But I guess it would be hypocritical for a guy in his position to pretend he didn't know what the pills he was peddling were used for. That didn't mean I had to like him.

"Is *Star Maker* a particularly good market?"

"Outstanding," he said. A little too chipper for me. "To start the season, they bring like a hundred and fifty singers out here. And a lot of those chicks don't make it through from the audition rounds because of their voices, if you know what I mean."

I took a deep breath. Whitey was watching me carefully.

"And once we get to the finals, the crowd is full of girlies. Every week, twice a week."

"Who do you sell to?"

"We're just talking about roofies here, right?" I nodded in confirmation. I didn't care about the rest of his inventory. "The crew guys, of course," Bumper said. "Coop, he's probably my best customer. He told me you already had this conversation with him, so I'm not giving away any secrets here."

"Who else?"

"Let's see," said Bumper, looking around the auditorium. "That guy." He pointed at the stage. "He bought a big batch couple a weeks ago."

I turned to where he was gesturing. Lenny Harris was hugging his daughter Patsy right by the footlights. Her head was nestled against his chest. She looked jubilant. His face was oddly flushed, red and white in splotches. He had a big, goofy smile on his face as he rocked her from side to side.

Shit.

I turned back to Bumper. "You sure?"

"Dude," he said with assurance, "I never forget a face."

I looked at Whitey, who raised his eyebrows as if to say, *Ain't that a bitch.*

"All right, Bumper. Appreciate your candor. We're done."

"We are?" he asked delightedly. "Cool."

Whitey and I shuffled off in opposite directions and then reconnoitered at the back of the hall.

"You surprised?" Whitey asked. "Because I'm not. I had a bad feeling about that guy every time we saw him at that meeting."

"I just feel bad for Patsy," I said. "She's such a sweet kid and she was so jazzed about having her father back in her life."

"Well, let's go hold his feet to the fire."

"Hold on, Whitey," I said. "All we know now is that Lenny bought roofies. Same as L. A. Cooper and a lot of other people on this set. We still have to hook him up with Matt."

"Why don't we take him for a drive and sweat him?"

"I have a better idea," I said. "Can I borrow your cell?"

Information found and dialed the number for the pizza place. Don Walmsley happened to be sitting right there between delivery runs. The counterman put him on.

"Hey, Don," I said. "This is Jim McNamara, the detective who spoke to you a couple of days ago."

"Hi, Detective."

"Remember I asked you about that night at the hotel and the guy who took the pizza off you? You couldn't describe him too clearly. But I want you to think carefully, Don. Did he remind you of anyone on TV?"

During my hike I had thought of Don watching the tube in his apartment, about our society's crappy cultural touchstone and how connected the pizza delivery man seemed to be to it.

After a pause, Don said, "Yeah, now that you mention it, he looked kind of like Pat Sajak."

"You sure?"

"I've only been watching *Wheel of Fortune* my whole life. Yeah, I'm sure."

I hung up, satisfied. I knew any half-assed defense lawyer could decimate a witness like Don Walmsley during cross-examination. Fortunately, I didn't have to meet courtroom standards. I only had to convince myself.

CHAPTER 26

Roxie was busy with postproduction demands, so that night I went back to my room and listened repeatedly to Boz Scaggs sing "I Just Go." It was beautiful and understated, something those *Star Maker* kids would never understand. They had grown up with Whitney Houston and Christina Aguilera in an age of egregious melisma, when singing was oversinging.

I listened to Boz burble until I couldn't hear Ricky Tavares's "Gentle on Mind" anymore. I listened until Ricky wasn't on my mind at all.

The next morning Whitey picked me up for the early meeting. Our special guest trailed us over. Fortunately, Lenny was there. We approached him after the closing prayers and requested that he accompany us into the parking lot.

"What's this about, fellas?" he asked. We were standing about ten yards from the darkly tinted driver's-side window of Whitey's Escalade. Looking at the SUV, I pointed at Lenny. There was a double tap from the horn.

Whitey and I turned to look at Lenny like parents who had just gotten a very bad report card. "What?" he said. "What?"

"Sitting behind the wheel of that car," I said gravely, "is the pizza guy who delivered to Matt Hanes. We brought him over here this morning and asked him to honk if he recognized the guy who took the pizza off him the night Matt was killed."

Lenny looked from me to the car and back at me again. As the import of what I was saying sank in, his face collapsed into one of the saddest expressions I've ever seen on a human.

"Shit," he said, his voice quavering. "Aw, shit."

"We need to talk, Lenny," I said, flicking my head at Whitey. He took Lenny's arm and led him back downstairs into the nearly deserted meeting space. I walked over to the Escalade and opened the door.

"How'd it go?" Roxie asked. I nodded. "Lenny?" she asked sadly, as if she really didn't want to hear that.

"We're going to interrogate him for a while," I said. "I'll call you later."

She got out of the Escalade, gave me a quick but tender kiss and walked over to her Honda. I went back inside, where Lenny was already pleading his case to Whitey. I pulled over a folding chair to join them.

"I know this doesn't make it right," Lenny said emotionally, "but I did it to help my daughter. Lord knows, I hurt that kid plenty in my addiction. Never cared about anything but my own selfish self. And you know what?" His voice cracked. "She never stopped loving me, praying for me. And now she has a chance to accomplish something really special. And I just wanted to help her, you know?

But I fucked up." At this point, he broke down. It took a few seconds for him to recover. "Thing is, if I admit what I did, it will destroy a once-in-a-lifetime opportunity for my Patsy. And I can't live with that. I took so much from this kid already. I can't rob her of her best chance to succeed." He wiped his face with his sleeve.

"I feel so shitty. I mean, I did awful things in my addiction and never thought twice about them. But now that I'm sober, I have to live with my conscience. And I'm not used to that. I want to do what's right here, I have to put my daughter first, above everything. You understand?"

He looked pleadingly at me and Whitey. Apparently he didn't see the level of sympathy he was hoping for. His lower lip spasmed for a few seconds and Lenny began to sob, quietly at first and then in big wracking wails. As AA vets, Whitey and I were both pretty comfortable watching a grown man cry.

So, apparently, was the guy wiping down the counters in the kitchen. He flicked a switch in there and headed for the exit. "Make sure you guys turn off the lights and pull the door firmly closed when you're done," he called out to us with disinterest as if he heard ten weepy confessionals a day.

It took a while for Lenny to compose himself. "Aw, shit," he said plaintively. "I didn't mean to hurt that kid, I swear to God. But I owed people and I…oh, shit. I am such a fuckup." There was a brief resumption of tears and then the story began to pour out.

Lenny had gotten sober in prison, but when he had been paroled, some old companions emerged with him. For instance, a bad gambling habit. But because he was an unemployed deadbeat dad, recovering junkie and ex-con, the only person he could get to take his action was another Lompoc graduate, a Long Beach bookie named Archie Archuleta.

Lenny had a disastrous season betting college football. The bets kept getting bigger as his losses mounted and he tried to dig his way out. The whole time he was bragging about how his beautiful, talented daughter was going to win this season's *Star Maker*, you wait and see.

Finally, Archie approached him with a solution to both their problems. If Lenny could get his daughter to cooperate in Archie's plan to rig the results of *Star Maker*, to make sure a certain singer won, then Archie could forgive Lenny's debts. Nothing violent or illegal. Probably something as simple as finding out another contestant's plans for the night. Or maybe making sure a back door was left unlocked at a predetermined time.

To Lenny's credit, he refused to involve his daughter in this chicanery despite mounting pressure and intimidation from Archuleta and his goons. And then, suddenly, the pressure stopped.

A few days later Archie had another proposal. Lenny simply had to get rid of this Matt Hanes kid everyone was talking about and he had to do it quick, before the finals began and Hanes's popularity soared. In this scenario, Lenny's debts wouldn't be forgiven. But if he refused Archie this favor, then the papers were going to get juicy details about what kind of low-life father Patsy Harris had.

You know how much the press loves dirt like that. It would get reprinted all over the country. TV would pick it up. Then how many votes did Lenny think his precious daughter would get? How would he feel then when he cost her *Star Maker*?

"Archie wasn't bluffing either. He showed me a copy of the letter. My life looks really nasty when you boil it down to the bullet points," said Lenny. "So now I'm searching around for a way to knock Matt out of the competition. I hate what I'm doing, but what choice do I have?" He looked beseechingly at each of us. If he was hoping for commiseration, he wasn't getting it.

"I had met this guy Bumper a few times at the *Star Maker* studios and I knew he dealt roofies, which are supposed to knock people out. So I figure if I can just give Matt enough for a slight OD, that should work. The producers find out he's doing drugs, they're going to boot him, right? I swear to you I tried to be scientific about it, figure out his body weight and all that shit. I got the idea because Patsy and the kids were all joking about Matt's nightly pizza ritual: three slices before bed and one for breakfast. I took the powder to a chemist friend down in San Diego to make it palatable. He runs a meth lab.

"Seriously, I wasn't trying to hurt him. Not bad anyway. Patsy really liked him. I don't know what went wrong, but guys, listen, if you can't let me slide on this, can you at least wait eight weeks to turn me in? Or until Patsy gets voted off. Whichever comes first."

You have to admire the alcoholic spirit. We'll still be trying to bargain with the devil as he's dropping us into the lake of fire.

Whitey and I exchanged a glance.

"Uh, Lenny," I ventured. "You're sort of glossing over a key point here: After you drugged Matt, why did you put a pillow over his face and smother him?"

Lenny looked up with genuine shock. "What? What are you talking about?"

"The pillow, Lenny. Cause of death: asphyxiation."

"I didn't touch him with a pillow or anything else. I delivered the pizza with the cap pulled down over my face and then I split. I thought he died of a drug overdose." Hope lit up his face. "You mean he didn't?"

We went over the sequence of events several times. Lenny had lifted one of Patsy's room cards earlier in the day. He intercepted the pizza guy by waiting in a supply room just off the lobby and watching the elevators through a crack. He took the pie to his daughter's room, distributed the drug more or less evenly and then microwaved the pizza before delivering it. Matt's door was open when he knocked. Patsy had said it always was except when he was asleep. No one else was in Matt's room when he took the pizza; no one Lenny noticed in the corridor or on his way out.

He was certain Archie hadn't sent backup. The bookie had made it clear from the beginning this was Lenny's task to perform, and besides, Lenny had never told Archie when or where he planned to act.

Which left us with most of the case solved. We had the guy who drugged the pizza. We knew a bookie in Long Beach was trying to cook the results of *Star Maker*. We were pretty sure he was the guy behind the fax that blackmailed Shontika off the show.

All we were missing was who killed Matt.

Lenny was, of course, ecstatic to find out he was off the hook for murder. But his delight was somewhat tempered when we informed him that he still faced criminal charges and that he was going to have to tell Patsy about drugging Matt. Or else we would.

Whitey jotted down all his contact info and we left Lenny in the parking lot, looking pretty desolate. I hoped he had himself a good sponsor. He was going to need it.

Back at my hotel, there were four messages. One from my sponsor Chris just wanting to say hello. One from my mother telling me that a woman I barely knew—hell, a woman she barely knew—had died. That's my mom: always spreading the misery. There was one from Roxie, saying she had given my number to Bobby at his request. Hoped that was okay. Also she had to work through tonight's broadcast, but she hoped to come over to my hotel afterward. "Please don't have any company when I get there this time," she said playfully.

And finally there was a message from Bobby. He told me he had tracked down the woman he had been with on the night of Matt's death and that she would vouch for him. But he couldn't bring her to the studio tomorrow because she was working every night this week. He gave me her name, Tina, and the cocktail lounge where she was employed. "Now go find someone else to hassle, you prick," Bobby concluded.

I got in a strenuous workout—weights and cardio—had lunch and took a nap that afternoon. Wouldn't mind following that same schedule every day. I'm a good candidate for early retirement—every way but financially.

Whitey picked me up that evening and we drifted south on the 101 to look up Tina. She worked in a dank Tiki bar in Cargo City. They made the cocktail waitresses wear those tiny parachute skirts and fishnet stockings. The look was pretty wasted on the bar's hard-drinking clientele, but it was perfect for Tina.

Her hair was dyed white-blond and styled choppy chic. She didn't look old enough to be in the bar, although the hardness of her eyes suggested she had already experienced plenty. She had a nice figure, although you got the impression it was a fluke of youth and wasn't going to last long. Tina seemed to know she was peaking and was pissed off that this was as good as it was going to get.

She wasn't too thrilled to see us, especially after we both ordered diet Cokes. But she consented to sit with us during her break.

"So," I said, "Bobby Turner."

"Yeah, I met him at Raffles, a club in Hollywood. Near Hollywood anyway," she said, reaching down to rub her calf.

"And?"

"And we went back to his hotel after the club closed. I was there until the morning."

"How long were you with him?"

"All night. He hit on me as soon as I walked in the door at Raffles, which was, what? Before ten? We danced, we drank, we laughed. He can be a funny guy when he's trying."

"And he was in your sight the whole night?"

"Except when one of us went to the bathroom, yeah."

"Anyone see you guys together?"

"Yeah, I came in with a group of friends. I can give you their names."

"And you're sure this was January seventeenth?"

"Well, I'm not too good with dates, but I know it was the night we're talking about."

"How?"

"He kept talking about how he was celebrating because he just found out he was a finalist on *Star Maker* and if I played my cards right, I could sleep with America's next big star. How he was going to be ten times bigger than Terry Taylor. And then a few days later, there Bobby was on the TV. Course, he wasn't calling me by then," she said. Glancing up at one of the sets bracketed over the bar, she continued, "Speaking of *Star Maker*, what the hell is wrong with that girl?"

Whitey and I both looked up. The show was on and Neveah was belting out her number. She looked even worse on-screen, like an extra in a zombie movie with brains spilling out its eye sockets.

"That's it?" I pressed. "Matt told you he just got on *Star Maker*?"

"That and the fact that it was Wednesday. The only night I have off, at least since Hal took over as manager," she said, staring daggers at a heavy bald man who resembled Peter Boyle sitting in a booth near the register.

Tina didn't seem like an ironclad alibi for Bobby by any means. But she wasn't through yet either.

"Oh, and the final thing," she said, checking her mouth in a compact she produced from somewhere on her person. "When I got up the next morning, there were cops in the hall, down in the lobby, everywhere in that hotel. The girl in the next room who was peeking out the door at the same time as me said one of the *Star Maker* contestants had been killed. So that's how I know."

"Did any of the police interview you?"

"No, I slipped out the fire staircase. I didn't want to lose my whole day answering stupid questions. Besides, I don't know nothing. Oh, look, there's Bobby!"

I thanked her and tipped her lavishly.

"She's a piece of work, huh?" Whitey said in the car as we drove off.

"Yeah, but one with enough detail to stand up as a witness," I noted. "I was kind of hoping to hang this on Bobby."

Whitey considered this as he drove. "Maybe we could shift our suspicions to Brian Breeze," he suggested.

"Ah, you're cheering me up already."

I deliberated over this mystery back in my room. I tried to summon up all the various personalities involved, the reasons for killing Matt, the window of opportunity, and then I sat quietly and let them collide in my head. It was a regular demolition derby.

I'm not one of those ratiocinating marvels like Sherlock Holmes or Hercule Poirot who can apply daunting logic to a problem until it is solved. My approach is to toss the pieces of the puzzle into the hopper and then turn off my mind. Let my subconscious work on it and hope like hell that inspiration strikes.

In my quiescent state, I pondered Matt's death. This process went on a lot longer than I intended. When I glanced over at the alarm clock, it was 10:20. That surprised me. One thing I had noticed about Roxie, she was consistently early for everything. She made punctual look tardy. I gave it a few more minutes and then I called her cell. It went right to a network notice, not even Roxie's message. And she always had her cell phone on.

I called Whitey, hoping he might have heard from her.

"Let me call my friend Joanie who works for Tootsi Frootsi, see if anyone knows anything," he said.

I don't do waiting well. It's like a bed of nails to me. How the hell are you supposed to get comfortable with that? I banged around the room restlessly, opening drawers, playing with the blinds. Stand up, sit down, fight, fight, fight. When the phone went off, I picked it up during the first ring.

It was a very terse Whitey. "Roxie left at nine. She told one of the other girls she was going home to change and then she had a date. I tried her house and her cell again. No answer. What do you want to do?"

"Sit tight for a while. Let's give it until midnight. Then we'll start to panic."

"Call me as soon as you hear something," he said.

When the phone rang about eight minutes later, I beat my own record, grabbing it while the sound was still a rumor. I was praying it was Roxie, with some quotidian excuse, like a flat tire.

A man's harsh voice demanded, "Jim McNamara?" Expectations are a killer. My heart plunged.

"Yeah."

"We have your girlfriend."

"Who is this?"

"Shut up and listen. You drop *Star Maker* right now. You don't act on what you know. You don't talk to anybody about what you know. You call up the producers and tell them you're quitting. If you do that, maybe this pretty girl will be okay."

"How do I—"

"Shut up, I tole you! If you don't do ezactly like I tole

you, you won't even recognize her. We're watching everything you do. You call those fuckers and quit. You won't hear from me again."

"Wait," I barked, "I need to talk to her."

"Fuck you," the voice said. Then I was listening to a dial tone.

I squeezed my temples with my right hand, took a couple of deep breaths and called Whitey. "They abducted Roxie."

I expected him to ask, *Who's they?* Instead he responded, "I'll be right over. Meet me downstairs."

Twenty minutes later he swerved into the driveway and fishtailed to a stop in front of the entrance. Before the car had stopped rocking on its suspension, I climbed in. Whitey was wearing an expression of angry determination I had never seen on him before. In fact, I didn't know he possessed a look like that. But at that moment, I was glad I didn't owe him money.

"Tell me what he said...exactly."

I recounted the conversation word for word.

"So what do we know that this guy doesn't want us to talk about? Only that some mook from Long Beach is trying to fix the contest." He was strangling the steering wheel.

"We need to have a talk with Lenny," I said.

Whitey threw the car in gear and mashed the accelerator. "On the phone, Whitey," I screamed as we rocketed out into the street. "On the freaking phone."

I braced myself as Whitey made the brakes squeal. He pulled against the curb, the car rocking in place. Pulling a slip of paper out of his shirt pocket, he stabbed a number emphatically into his cell.

"Lenny," he said, "this is Whitey. You know who I am? Good. Did you call your bookie friend Archuleta after we talked this morning?... Why would you want to do something stupid like that?... Because that scumbag has kidnapped one of my favorite people, asshole, that's why."

He listened for a few seconds, seething. "I'm not interested in your sorry excuses. You don't owe Archuleta anything, you shithead. But I promise you this: If he harms one hair on my friend's head, you're going to wish they never let you out of that prison cell, you understand me?

"Now give me his address... Archuleta's, asshole, who do you think?... Then give me that one and you better pray that he's there." Whitey scrawled an address on the same piece of paper, followed by the initials "L.B." He looked like he was about to thumb off the phone then he brought it to his mouth again.

"You warn Archuleta we're coming for him and I will fuck you up worse than you can imagine. The only call I want you to make after I hang up is to your daughter. You keep talking about how you want to do right by her? Well, start with the truth, so she can begin dealing with her real father, not this fantasy she has going in her head. Do it now, asshole, before you damage her any more."

He hung up and turned to me. "I have Archuleta's address," he said, roaring away from the curb. "At least his office address. We'll start there."

He hit the entrance ramp to the freeway doing close to eighty. "Lenny called Archuleta as soon as he got back to his hotel this morning. I said, 'Why would you do something stupid like that?' He said, 'Because Archie will hurt me a lot worse than you guys ever would. You don't understand,' he says. 'Archie has been trying to get this scam together for three years.'" Whitey swerved across two lanes on the 101 to outflank a panel van and a Honda, both of which were doing about seventy. The way we passed them, it felt like they were parked.

"He said, 'There's more money involved in this scheme than you could ever dream of.'"

"But why Roxie?" I asked.

"My theory is that JoJo must be part of this. She saw Roxie come by your room the other night and figured out there was something going on between you two. She must have told Archuleta and he grabbed her to shut us up."

"Do we know if Roxie is being held at this address?" I said, holding up the paper.

Whitey shook his head. "It's the only address Lenny had for him. But Lenny says he keeps late hours."

As we flashed up onto the 405, Whitey turned on the CD player. He had queued it up to Creedence Clearwater's "Heard It Through the Grapevine," which he played at top volume all the way down to Long Beach. I guess it was his psych music. I have to say, until I heard it that night, under those circumstances, with Whitey burning a hole in the windshield with his eyes, I never realized how menacing and brutal that song could be.

I should make it clear: I was terrified for Roxie's safety and determined to do anything I had to in order to win her freedom. But Whitey's fury was so overwhelming, so palpable, it even scared me. Both literally and figuratively, I felt like a passenger on this search-and-destroy mission.

With the help of the car navigator, we found Archuleta's office. It was an unmarked storefront in a small battered strip mall about two blocks off the docks in Long Beach. There was no street traffic, no one was parked in the strip lot, and none of the adjoining businesses—a Chinese take-out, a Radio Shack, a barbershop and a grimy party supply store—was open.

The plate-glass windows in Archie's place were painted sky-blue, or maybe that was a tinted film applied to the glass. But you couldn't see inside. It was the type of setup that on the East Coast would be a car service or a social club. It was obvious, from where we were parked across the street from the lot, that the lights were on.

"I'm going to do a little reconnoitering," said Whitey, leaning over his seat to rummage through a big plumber's bag in the back. He got out, palming a device, and walked away toward the back of the car.

The next time I saw him, he was slipping around the side of the building and padding up to Archie's door in a crouch. Getting to his knees on the darker side of the entrance away from the other businesses, he slowly threaded a tube that looked like one of those snaky reading lights into the narrow space where light was spilling out from under the door.

Whitey worked the tube as he scrutinized the small green night-light display screen it was attached to. A minute later, the screen went dark and Whitey began withdrawing the tube ever so slowly. He pushed up onto his toes and quietly scooted around the corner.

Then he was opening the front door of the car and sliding in. "Okay, there are two cars parked behind the building. Three guys in the front room. No sign of Roxie. There's a small storage room in the back and a bathroom, but I think they're empty. Here's what we're going to do, and we have to synchronize this. I'm going to walk up and knock on the door. Two beats later you're going to crash this car through the front window."

"Whoa. What?"

"Distraction technique, bud. Very effective."

"Can't I do my Johnny Mathis imitation? That's very distracting. This is an expensive car, Whitey."

"It's a loaner. Now, look, when I get out, I want you to pull slowly into the lot and park facing Archuleta's store. Keep the headlights doused. When you see me drop my hand like this," he said, executing a starter's motion, "I want you to floor it and torpedo the store midships. Whatever you do, don't hit me. And keep your seat belt fastened. Once you've penetrated the wall, jump out fast, because I'm going to need your help...You ready?"

That seemed to be a rhetorical question, because he was already opening the door. "Let's do this," he said, climbing out.

I tried to follow his directions to the letter. I rolled across the street and backed into a spot across from the store about fifteen yards away. To avoid a support column for the mall's sidewalk overhang, I had to aim slightly to the right of center. I sat with the engine idling and my hands tightly clutching the wheel.

Whitey walked up to the door and looked back at me. He lifted his chin in inquiry. I nodded that I was ready. He raised a fist by the door, and saluted me with his other open hand. He began to subtly bob in place, catching a rhythm. Then he knocked twice, took a step back toward me and dropped his arm.

I jammed the gas pedal to the floor and the Escalade roared forward. I remember a brief weightless sensation, like I was holding on to the steering wheel for dear life. The rest went by in a flash. The front wheels hit the four-inch-high cement parking strip in the lot and bucked in the air. They bounced, hit the curb and flew up even higher.

There was movement off to my left as Whitey launched himself at the door. But as the front end of the Escalade rose, all I could see in front of me was the hood. I felt like I was in the saddle on a rearing horse. Hiyo, Silver!

It was as if the car had been catapulted through the window, shattering it like Daryl Dawkins taking down a backboard. The Escalade's front end was in the office, along with a lot of debris, but the back wheels hit the wall beneath the window and stuck. I couldn't see through the windshield, which was covered with dust and fracture webs, but I heard the tires screaming and took my foot off the gas. A loud clapper alarm was going off insistently. The car briefly seesawed in the window casement and then settled on its front tires.

I jumped out and looked around. To my left, Whitey was scuffling with a bull-necked guy holding a pistol. In front of me sat a dusky guy with a magnificently wrinkled face. He was staring transfixed at the front of the car, which had come to rest with its bumper nestled against his desk. His greased-back hair had come loose on either side of his head. That along with the look of dumb shock on his face made him resemble a Mexican Shemp Howard.

To my right, a younger, more athletic-looking guy in a track suit was down on his knees on the floor, shaking his head and grimacing.

Whitey had stepped inside the gunman's grasp so that they were facing the same direction like a dancing couple. He reached up and over with his right arm, pinning the guy's elbow to his side with his own. With his left hand, Whitey snared the wrist of the guy's gun hand and snapped it out and down while winching up on the elbow. There was a double crack as the forearm broke in two places. The guy dropped the gun, howling in agony.

Whitey released his wrist and whipped back his left hand, forming it into a fist as he mashed the guy's nose with his knuckles. There was the briefest pause, as the gunman's body seemed to absorb this latest assault. Then blood began gushing from his nostrils and streaming from the gash atop his flattened bridge.

Whitey stepped away and the guy went down. Whitey glanced past me at the other guard dog, who was just rising to his feet with a ferocious look on his face and reaching inside his track-suit top. Without looking, Whitey pointed across his body at the seated man and said, "Take care of Archie."

Then he flew by me. It was a move like you see in one of these new gravity-defying kung fu movies. Only Whitey wasn't being propelled by wires. And this was a guy who until that night I had never even seen walk fast. Now he was acting like Spider-Man.

He slid smoothly across the hood of the Escalade, on his right thigh, his left top foot slightly forward as if he were stealing second base. The foot caught Sporty Thug in the chest just as he was pulling out his gun. He stumbled back against the wall.

Before the thug could gather his balance, Whitey landed, took two nimble steps forward and kicked out and down with his left foot against the inside of the guy's right knee. There was a sickening snap of bone and tendon and the guy fell, a look of pained astonishment on his face.

At that point, I remembered my assignment. Luckily, Archuleta had also been absorbed in watching Whitey in action. But as I advanced on him, he began rooting around frantically in his desk. He was dredging the lower compartment as I came around behind him. I slammed the drawer shut with my foot. Archuleta tried to draw his arm out, but he wasn't quite fast enough.

He bellowed as I kept the pressure on. When Whitey walked over, I released. Archie lifted his swollen hand and stared at it, wincing. You could almost see it pulsing like the paw of some hapless cartoon cat. *"Ay, pendejo,"* he cursed.

"Is Roxie here?" Whitey demanded.

Archie looked at him contemptuously and spit. "Fuck you!"

Whitey reached over, grabbed him above the scruff of

the neck and slammed his face down onto the desk. When he lifted his head back up, Archie's face had a dozen or more glass shards embedded in it, remnants of the picture window.

"Is Roxie here?" Whitey repeated, quieter this time.

No answer. Whitey banged his head down again. More decorative glass clung on. His lips looked like a pebble-studded ashtray.

I saw movement off to the corner of my eye. El Toro had scrabbled around on the floor, picked up his pistol with his left hand, and had just leveraged himself onto his knees, facing the sidewalk. I planted my left foot and sweep-kicked him hard in the back of his head with my right. He seemed to fly forward, his chin hitting the floor with a loud thunk. He bounced once and settled. I nudged the pistol away from his unconscious hand with my foot.

"Is Roxie here?" Whitey was practically whispering by now. Still no answer. The alarm continued to scream.

Whitey merely tightened his grip and Archie shouted, "No! No! She's not here. You can see she's not here!"

"We have to go," Whitey said, lifting Archie up by his hair. "Get my bag from the back seat, Jim."

"Fuck you. I'm not going anywhere with you." Archie hadn't even finished speaking when Whitey gave him a quick chop in the Adam's apple. Archie began gagging uncontrollably, gasping for breath, tears running from his eyes.

Whitey yanked him around and pushed him toward the back door with a fistful of hair. I walked ahead, threw open the two bolts on the metal-plated door and we stepped into the back alley. The sound of distant but approaching sirens spiced the night air. Whitey reached in Archie's pants and tossed me a set of car keys. There was a Dodge Ram on the key chain. I headed for the red Durango.

"What about your car?" I asked.

"I think it's wedged in there," Whitey said. I threw Whitey's bag on the front seat, unlocked the SUV's doors and started the engine. Whitey pushed our passenger into the back seat and we were gone before the first police car arrived.

We drove about three miles along the waterfront and then Whitey told me to turn onto an overgrown frontage road by one of the docks. Half a mile down, there was a small brick relay station. Whitey told me to pull around back.

He pulled Archie out of the back seat roughly and forced him to kneel upright in the gravel turnaround. "Now we're going to ask some questions and you're going to answer them," Whitey said, going over to the passenger door and reaching in his bag for a roll of duct tape. "This can be very simple or it can be very painful. It's up to you."

Archie's head was tilted back as he tried to breathe. He regarded Whitey with his eyes wide and rolling back, like a horse that's just seen a snake.

"First and most importantly, where is Roxie?" As he asked this, he methodically began binding Archie's wrists together behind his back with tape. Every time he'd tear off a strip, you could see Archie flinch.

"She's at my cousin Gordo's. It's over on the east side."

"Good. We're making progress. Did you or one of your men kill Matt Hanes?"

Archie began shaking his head, sticking out his lower lip. "Unnh-unnh. No way. That's all on that limpdick Lenny."

"But you did get that black girl thrown off?"

Archie nodded.

"Where did you get her criminal record?"

"Let's just say it came from an interested party."

"Let's just say you tell me," said Whitey, lifting up the guys conjoined hands behind his back. As Archie's shoulder blades poked though his shirt, he began to scream.

"Okay, it was a friend in Phoenix."

"What's his name?" Whitey asked, pulling the hands an inch higher.

"Raphael Marcado. His name's Raphael Marcado," said Archie, the words coming out in a rush. Whitey let up on his arms. "Raphael got me started. He's the one bankrolled my book. If I pull off this *Star Maker* deal, I can have all of Tucson. Hell, I could have Vegas."

Whitey looked at me over Archie's head. "You have any questions, Jim?"

"Yeah, who is it you're trying to install as the next *Star Maker* winner?"

"I can't tell you that," he said. Whitey yo-yoed his arms up and down twice.

"Fuck! All right, stop doing that," he fumed. "It's JoJo Johnson. Raphael has a big hard-on for her. Me, I only care about all the money I'm going to win on her. She was two-fifty-to-one last week. You try getting those odds at the racetrack."

"Last question: Do you have someone working for you inside the show?"

"No," he said stubbornly. I looked at Whitey, who began to slowly crank up the hands. "Oh, shit...shit...SHIT! All right, yes. I do."

"Who?" Whitey tapped his hands up. A gentle reminder.

"Bobby Turner," he said bitterly. "It had to be somebody who could last until the very end and then throw it. What good does it do you if your fix gets eliminated in week three? So I picked Bobby. But that's why we had to get rid of Matt Hanes first. Bobby was afraid they would split the little-girl vote. But if Matt was gone, he would have a clear shot to the final two. Then JoJo would win, Bobby would still get a record contract as the runner-up. And no one would ever find out about the arson that burned up his family when he was fourteen."

Whitey and I looked at each other.

"Okay, Archie, we're done here," Whitey said. "Let's go over to the east side."

Whitey used Archie's cell phone to call the bookie's cousin, Gordo. He held the phone up to the bookie's mouth while Archie instructed Gordo to untie the girl and bring her out on the porch.

We pulled up about thirty yards from Gordo's bungalow under a streetlight. Roxie was standing with her hand to her mouth behind a corpulent Mexican in baggy blue-jean cutoffs.

We got out and I waved for Roxie to join us. Archie, his arms still bound behind him, nodded at Gordo, who stepped aside. Roxie ran toward us, beginning to cry.

Whitey gave Archie a shove and he stumbled forward. "We'll leave your car in the lot at the Staples Center."

Roxie ran into my arms and hugged me tightly. Then she looked up at me and Whitey, and wiping her eyes, laughing and crying at the same time, asked, "What took you guys so long?"

"Ask Spider-Man over here," I said, tilting my head at Whitey, my new hero.

CHAPTER
29

Roxie asked if she could spend the night with me, so Whitey dropped us off at the hotel. I had a bunch of questions about how he had transformed from Mr. 12-Step to Mr. 1200 Stitches in one night. But he asked if we could talk about it another time. The last words I said to him were, "I've seen a side of you tonight I didn't know existed."

By the next day, I could have used the same line on Roxie. When we got up to my room, she was exhausted and wrung out—though thankfully unhurt except for a minor rope burn. She took a long shower and put on an oversized De La Soul T-shirt of mine.

She lay down next to me under the covers, nuzzled up against my shoulder, sighed, "Oh, boy," and was out like a light. After a few minutes, when she was breathing deeply, I pulled away so I could watch her sleep. I found myself smiling. She looked so beautiful and so peaceful. I could have glanced all night.

I must have fallen asleep eventually, because when I awoke, there was sunlight streaming in the windows and the situation was reversed: Roxie was looking down on me and smiling. While her hand stroked me to life.

She kicked the sheets with the back of her foot and they ballooned up in the air. She hopped over on top of me and the covers settled softly down and around her with a gentle caress of air. She reached down and guided me inside her, biting her lower lip in concentration. Then she began to rock on top of me, slowly at first. We moaned simultaneously when she blossomed open, a synchronicity that made us look at each in wonder.

She closed her eyes as she began moving faster, and with more urgency. I noticed the muscles in her body start to clench and she began again to bite her lower lip. Then her head rose up and her mouth opened, as if there were a song of terrible beauty that had to escape her. Her chest was heaving. There was a crescendo of four cries, then she shivered for a long moment and toppled onto my chest.

After she caught her breath, we rolled over and I began to move atop her. I wanted to prolong this feeling, but she was stroking my lower back and looking up at me, her eyes smoldering. Then she cupped my cheeks and began to pull me into her with each stroke. What can I say? My cup ranneth over.

Afterward, we showered together. The water and soap running over Roxie's skin made her shine in the golden morning light. Oh, to be a painter.

I kidded her about how quickly she had come. "Is that the way it is with country girls?" I asked, washing her calf.

"I think it had more to do with me being kidnapped," she said, looking back and down at me, the water sluicing off her hair and running down her sleek back in rivulets.

"There's nothing like the threat of death to make you feel really alive."

We drank some coffee and scoured the paper, but there was no mention of our escapade in Long Beach.

Then we made love again. And this time, I was kidnapped.

We took a taxi to Roxie's house so she could change and retrieve her car. That afternoon, we met Mitch Reynolds over at the production office in Universal City. He assured Whitey that the car, the property damage and any and all legal charges would be taken care of by the network lawyers.

"They're entertainment lawyers," pointed out Roxie. "Do they handle criminal affairs?"

"They work for Fox. It's all criminal, honey," Mitch said.

When Rodney and Ian showed up, we explained the conspiracy to install JoJo as the next *Star Maker* winner and of Bobby's hand in making that happen.

"They have to go. It's as simple as that," said Ian, who seemed unusually sober and rather distressed to find himself in such a state.

"We can't screw up the production schedule," said Mitch.

"Then we'll let them go one at a time, victims of a fickle voting audience," said Ian. "Bobby first. He goes tonight. I don't want him sticking around another week as a lame duck. I'm rather afraid of the damage he might do."

"We'll never get that together in time for tonight's show," protested Rodney.

"It will mean recutting a lot of the segments and editing a valedictory salute to Bobby," said Ian, gesturing to his assistant. "I'll alert the studio. Get them started."

"Oh, my God," said a poleaxed Rodney. "I just realized what this will do to an already meager talent pool. At least

JoJo and Bobby were good-looking. How in God's name am I going to promote Eva or Flip as the next Star?" He shuddered.

Ian, who was busily giving orders on the phone, put his hand over the speaker to interject, "You'll just have to whip up another silk purse, dear boy. You should be quite used to it by now."

They all began barking into phones. The scene reminded me of the first time I had met them. It seemed as good a time as any to withdraw. As Whitey, Roxie and I headed for the door, Mitch called out, "I'm just so glad we got this thing straightened out. Good work, McNamara."

Ian and Rodney tore themselves away from their conversations to add their approbation.

It could have been a satisfying moment of professional triumph, except for one thing: We still didn't know who had killed Matt. But this didn't seem like a propitious time to point that out.

Over dinner at a sushi restaurant, I pressed Whitey to explain where he had learned to be so lethal.

Looking down at his hands, he began to talk. "I was a full-blown alcoholic by the time I was thirteen, the latest in a long line of dumbass drunks in my family. But other than massacring most of my brain cells, there were no real serious consequences. Then I killed that college student speeding down Ventura Boulevard in a blackout.

"Suddenly I was facing a long jolt in a state penitentiary. I can't tell you how terrified I was at that prospect. All I had heard my whole life was that prison was a sodomy circus. And a handsome young kid like me would be passed around like a rental tool until I was toothless and haggard.

"I had four months until I had to check into my new home and I determined I would make myself into a badass, the likes of which even a convict would cower from. And

I asked all over the Southland: What is the most vicious fighting style there is? I ended up with a little guy named Jimmy Wang. He had a tiny dojo in a strip mall in Irvine, not unlike the one we visited last night where Archuleta kept his book.

"Jimmy taught kenpo karate to classes of overweight eight-year-old kids. But it was rumored he knew much more. He agreed to teach me a style he called extreme estrima. It was basically Philippino street fighting combined with a little kickboxing and a dash of cappo. I studied with Jimmy every hour he had available. The idea is to inflict maximum damage on your opponent. It's designed for people who expect to be consistently overmatched in battle, as I was in prison."

He looked up at us and tried to smile. But he wasn't selling it.

I tried to lighten the mood. "Man, that one move where you pulled the guy's arms up behind his back, that was fiendish."

"Oh, that wasn't estrima. I learned that in yoga. They actually try to get you to do that pose. It's killer."

"Do you still train for martial arts?" Roxie asked.

"Not nearly as much as I should," Whitey said. "I go through some of the routines at half speed once in a while. But there's no one to study with, basically. Jimmy was one of a kind. I think he made most of that stuff up."

"Well, I can't tell you how grateful I was to have you by my side last night. Wait, scratch that. I was grateful to have you five feet in front of me, beating the shit out of those guys."

"They brought it on themselves," he said. "Shouldn't have messed with Roxie."

She and Whitey toasted with glasses of cranberry juice.

We headed over to the studio for what would be my final results show.

This time, when Brian Breeze recapped the results, he pulled over Neveah and Flip to stand by him as the lowest vote-getters. There were gasps from the audience when Brian asked Bobby to join them. Bobby wasn't too happy about it either. I think he saw the writing on the wall.

He kept staring around angrily, at the judges, at Brian, at me, trying to find someone to appeal to. At the next commercial break, he grabbed the mic from Breeze and made his pitch to the director. "Come on, Stan," he shouted. "This isn't right. You know it's not right. You send me packing and you got a long season of nothing. Look at the shitbirds on this stage." He gestured at his housemates. "You need me and you know it. Come on, man."

Bobby's soliloquy got the crowd buzzing, but there was silence from the booth. And so the show moved on to its inevitable conclusion. Bobby didn't go quietly, but he did go. Neveah, who still looked like a giant locust, was giddy at having dodged a bullet.

But she was the only happy one on that stage. I'd never seen a more disconsolate group of survivors. I guess they could sense the *Star Maker* franchise crumbling down around them.

I thought for a moment that Patsy too had been infected with Eva's pinkeye, but on closer regard, I realized her red orbs were more organic. She looked like someone who had been crying for hours. I surmised that Lenny, who was not in attendance, had summoned up the courage to tell her what he had done.

After the long night in Long Beach I was exhausted and went back to the hotel to sleep. The next morning, there was an article in *USA Today* by Dan Rubowski in which he agonized over the *Star Maker* results. What do the surprise dismissals of Shontika and Bobby Turner in consecutive weeks signify? Is there a shift in the zeitgeist? What do the show's voters want? Dan had five meaty theories.

I got a good chuckle over that before I headed up to the studio to meet Roxie. We were going camping for the weekend in Will Rogers State Park and she had gone home to pack some supplies.

I watched the eight remaining finalists fight over Bee Gees songs until Roxie showed up. "No Rodney this week?" I asked, after kissing her.

"No, he's off playing golf."

"I can't imagine he's too happy having the Brothers Gibb on the docket."

"Actually, he didn't make much of a stink. I think he's a closet Maurice fan. But he does keep pushing Sandy for ELO night. Why do I think you had a hand in that?"

I smiled at her. She had been studying my CD collection. I liked that.

"I have to check on something with Joanie before we leave," Roxie said. "And I'm parked over by her office. So why don't I meet you outside the studio entrance in five?"

I got out there a little early. When Flip launched into "I Started a Joke," I simply couldn't bear it. I was standing outside the door when Rodney's friend George Oglesby came out in a tropical shirt that only served to make him look more pasty.

"Cheers, George," I said.

"Hallo."

"What are you doing here?"

"Thought I might run into Rodney."

"Ah," I said knowingly. "You much of a golfer, George?"

"Me? No, I despise the game."

"That's funny, isn't it? That one friend would grow up to hate a sport that the other friend was so slavishly devoted to."

"Pardon?"

I turned up my palm, surprised that he wasn't getting me. "You know: you hating golf while Rodney is mad about it."

"Rodney?"

"Yes. He's a golf nut."

"Rodney has never picked up a golf club in his life. He hates the game far more than I do." As George walked away, he looked back over his shoulder at me as if I were quite daft.

Just then, Roxie pulled up to the curb, her Lego car laden with gear. "Let's go camping," she said enthusiastically.

"Change of plans," I said, getting in.

CHAPTER
31

I can't believe I never checked on the whereabouts of the judges," I said once Whitey had joined us at my hotel. "I was so focused on the kids, I never gave it a thought."

"Shouldn't we be looking at L. A. Cooper first?" asked Whitey. "He's the one with a pocket full of roofies."

"Except roofies aren't what killed Matt," I said. "It's whoever walked into his room afterwards and strangled him."

"I still don't believe it was Rodney," said Roxie. "Matt was the best singer we had. I can't see Rodney doing something that would damage his livelihood."

"All I know is that Rodney has been consistently lying about where he's going. He passes himself off as a regular Tiger Woods. And the guy has never picked up a club in his life. That makes him a suspect in my book."

Whitey nodded. He seemed rather downcast again. I suspect that violent episode in Long Beach had brought back a chapter in his life that he didn't enjoy visiting.

"What's the name of Rodney's assistant?"

"Shannon."

"Do you have her cell?"

"Yes."

"Call her on the landline. I'll put it on speakerphone."

Roxie retrieved the number from her cell and dialed it. Shannon picked it up on the second ring. "Hello?"

"Hey, Shannon. It's Roxie."

"You sound kind of echoey. Do you have me on speakerphone?"

"Yeah."

"Who's there with you?" she asked warily.

"Jim McNamara and Whitey Stahl. You've met them."

"Yeah."

"Hey, Shannon. It's Jim. Where are you right now?"

"Uhm, I'm right outside Beverly Greens. I'm waiting for Rodney to finish his round."

"I know you're trying to cover for him, but we need to speak with Rodney right now. Face-to-face. Where is he?"

"Shit," she said, drawing out the sibilance. "Look, you don't understand...."

"I don't want to understand. Shannon. This is a matter of life and death. Where is he?" She hesitated. "Do you want me to have Mitch Reynolds call you?"

"At 1858 Wilshire," she finally said. "Apartment six."

"I thought Rodney lives in the Hills," said Roxie.

"He keeps this apartment too."

"Okay, thanks," I said.

"I am so fired," she said, hanging up.

We had to unload the tent and a hibachi to get Whitey in the back seat of Roxie's Honda before we could set off. Whitey was still without wheels.

The building on Wilshire turned out to be a compact terraced apartment in an office neighborhood. No doorman. Rather low-rent by Rodney's standards.

Apartment six was at the far end of the building on the second floor. As we approached the door, we heard a woman screaming, "No, no! Please stop it."

Whitey said, "We're going in." He backed as far as he could against the railing and poised himself to spring at the door.

Roxie held up a hand. "Wait a sec," she said, reaching for the knob. She turned it and the door swung open.

The woman's screams got louder and more piercing. "Oh, my God. Please stop!"

I ran in first, with Whitey and Roxie on my heels. Through the living room, furnished as if from a catalogue—or by an assistant with a catalogue—and into what should have been the dining room. But there was no table or chairs. The blinds and the curtains were drawn, the only light provided by dozens of candles scattered around the room.

Along the wall, what appeared to be a moving pad was affixed to the wall. And the figure of a man was grinding a screaming female into it. I hit the light switch.

There were restraints attached to the wall and the woman was attached to three of them. The man had her free arm in a half nelson that he was pushing at an alarming angle up her back. The man was dressed in a terribly tight pair of leather shorts with suspenders and nothing else. His back and legs bristled with so much black hair, at first I thought he was a werewolf.

As soon as the light came on, the woman went quiet. "What the bloody hell?" spluttered the man, turning to face us angrily. It was Rodney.

Spread-eagled against the wall, her makeup smeared,

was Sugar Kane, dressed in the cheerleader's outfit that had once made her famous.

"Jesus," said Roxie, involuntarily turning away, revolted at this tableau.

"What the hell do you people think you're doing here?" Rodney insisted.

"Lovely day for golf, innit?" said Whitey. With that comment, Rodney seemed to sag.

"Whatever it is you've come to do, please get it over with and then get the hell out," said our host, making a last feeble attempt at preserving his dignity.

"We need to talk with you, Rodney. And we need your undivided attention."

"Then do so."

"Would you mind unshackling her?" Whitey asked.

"Oh, for God's sake," said an exasperated Rodney, kneeling to untie Sugar.

When he was finished, we all stood facing each other. It was an awkward moment. "How about we adjourn to the living room?" suggested Roxie.

Rodney blew out his lips and then extended his hand in a mock bow, inviting us to go first. And so we sat—Whitey, Roxie and myself squeezed on one couch and Sugar and Rodney across from us—she in her ridiculously juvenile outfit, he in his Tyrolean S&M scoutmaster getup.

"Whenever you're ready," he said, glaring at me.

"Where were you the night Matt Hanes was killed? And I must warn you: playing golf is not an acceptable answer."

I watched disbelief and then indignation wash over his face. "Are you bloody serious?" he shouted. "That's what this is about? You barge in here to ask me if I killed Matt?" He shook his head. "All right, I'll answer your question. It so happens that was the night of our annual boys' night out. Brian and L.A. and I go out each year at the beginning of the season, hit the strip clubs, drink to oblivion and tell each other lies. They can both vouch for me. As can half the strippers in L.A. Satisfied? Good. You're fired." He even did the little Donald Trump hand gesture as he said it. One reality TV star paying homage to another.

But no one was looking at or listening to Rodney. We were all staring at Sugar. She had been sitting there, rubbing her elbow and smiling blankly, as if we were all at a Tupperware party. But as soon as I asked the big question, she fell back on the couch as if shot by an arrow. As Rodney fulminated, she sat as if catatonic, her eyes unfocused, all the color draining from her face.

"How about you, Ms. Kane?" Her eyes didn't move.

"That's quite enough," interjected Rodney.

But I pressed on. "Did you go to Matt Hanes's hotel room that night?"

She looked at me forlornly. "I..."

For the first time, Rodney looked over at her and saw her crestfallen face. "Oh, God, Sugar, don't tell me you were sleeping with that ponsey little boy." She turned her head slowly to look at him but did not speak.

"Why don't you tell us what happened when you got there?" I asked.

Her head tracked back to me. "I went over because he was flirting with me. They all want me." She looked at Roxie for confirmation. "He was wasted when I got there, But I had gone to so much trouble, getting all dolled up, sneaking in the side of the hotel with a big floppy hat. They make such a big deal of me socializing with the contestants. And that's so wrong. There's so much I can teach them.

"And so I decided to go for it with Matt. Because once they get in the house it's harder to get any time alone with them. So he was lying on the bed and I slipped off my coat and underneath I was wearing the cutest little miniskirt and a see-through belly shirt with a frilly blue bra underneath... and he started to laugh at me. To laugh. Like I was ridiculous. And I said, 'Don't you want me, Matt?' And he laughed even harder."

Sugar's gentle kneading of her elbow grew more forceful as she talked. At this point she was angrily rubbing it. "I told him to stop. Stop! But he kept laughing. I put my hands over my ears, but I could still hear him. So I picked up the pillow on his bed and I held it over his mouth. But I could still hear him. I pressed down harder and harder. And then I picked up my coat and put on my hat, but all the way down the stairs, I could still hear that laughter."

I looked over at Rodney, who was staring at Sugar with his mouth open. There were a lot of emotions on display in his face. But I could swear at least one of them was heartbreak.

I didn't stick around to the end of the season. My job was over, so I headed home. I asked Roxie if she'd like to come back to Connecticut with me, but she said she had moved to L.A. for a career, not a boyfriend, and she wanted to keep working it. So we're trying the long-distance thing for now.

Star Maker had to change on the fly, so Sugar was replaced by a local, a Los Angeles radio personality named Angie DeGuzman. She disagreed with everything Rodney said. Everyone agreed it was a good fit. Her hot Latin fire, his cold British disdain.

The press speculated that Sugar had gone away to deal with a serious physical ailment. The constant injuries she kept showing up with were symptoms, it was maintained, of a debilitating joint disorder that she had bravely tried to soldier through.

Before I left, I did get a peek at Ian's vaunted prediction. On the day I went by the office to pick up my check, I opened up the envelope when no one was watching. No name was written down. In a spidery script, it simply read: "I need stronger vodka."

I'm sure that when that envelope was opened with fanfare at the season wrap party, the winner's name would be printed there with certitude in a manly assistant's handwriting.

Roxie kept me posted on the backstage intrigue as the *Star Maker* finalists dwindled to a precious few. Right up until the final week, there was more backstabbing on that show than at a Borgia family reunion. Cletus was the victim of wardrobe sabotage when his pants embarrassingly split during a live show, the cap to John Denver week. Later it was discovered that someone had meticulously removed the threading.

Then *Access Hollywood* and the other entertainment shows somehow got a tape of a party at the *Star Maker* house that no one was aware was being recorded. Greg, who didn't seem to have a sense of humor, turned out to be an incredible mimic. He did devastating imitations of L.A., Rodney and even Angie. After that aired, the judges turned on him and then the voters.

Eva had a special homeopathic solution she gargled with before performing. Someone slipped boric acid into her potion during Guess Who theme week after which Eva could barely croak out the words to "These Eyes." In my heart, I hoped that was Neveah getting her revenge.

And as to the eventual winner, well, Roxie just sent me his new CD. You can say what you want about Ricky Tavares, but the guy sings a mean "Good King Wenceslas."